TRAVIS: FIREBRAND COWBOYS

BARB HAN

TORJAKE PUBLISHING

Copyright © 2023 by Barb Han

All rights reserved.

No part of this book may be reproduced in any form or by any electronic or mechanical means, including information storage and retrieval systems, without written permission from the author, except for the use of brief quotations in a book review.

Editing: Ali Williams

Cover Design: Jacob's Cover Designs

Proofreading: Judicious Revisions

To Brandon, Jacob, and Tori for being the great loves of my life. I don't know how I got so lucky to have each of you in my life but I know how truly blessed I am. To Babe for being my hero, my best friend, and my place to call home. I love you with all that I am.

1

Travis Firebrand stepped outside the front door of his small ranch-style home on Firebrand Cattle property and onto the porch. Hands on his hips, he stared at the sight in front of him in disbelief. "I'll be damned."

What the hell was Brynne Beauden doing barreling toward his home in her old Chevy, kicking up a dust storm the size of an F1 tornado? He'd be amused if it wasn't for the shotgun hanging out the driver's side window and the fact he'd experienced enough drama recently to last a lifetime.

What had he done to piss her off now? Breathe the wrong air?

Brynne's old Chevy skidded to a stop as the dust cloud enveloped her pickup.

"Stay away from my crops, Firebrand," Brynne managed to cough out as the dust filled her airways.

"What are you talking about?" Travis raked his fingers through thick, untamable hair and shot his I'd-rather-be-at-the-rodeo-than-right-here look. "I hate to disappoint you, seeing as how you're all fired up but haven't been anywhere near your corn."

Brynne emerged from the cloud wearing cowgirl boots and a pair of jeans that should be illegal on a curvy body like hers. They fit like a second skin, showing off the perfect S shape of her body. She'd been two years ahead of him in school and hadn't so much as given him a second glance in the hallways, except maybe to razz him about a missed catch on the baseball field. Her teasing words were the only ones she'd said directly to him during the two years they crossed over in high school.

Pranks were a different story.

He wasn't sure who started it—her, if memory served— but they'd played pranks on each other ever since he realized she was the one who put exploding glitter confetti in his locker. Those stopped too after she went off to community college.

And then they ran into each other a couple of months ago in downtown Austin. Her Chevy broke down on her, so he did the only thing he could do and helped her get the pickup running again. They'd spent one helluva a weekend together, after which she offered to buy him a beer as a thank you.

They never did have that beer but the sex had been the best of his life. He'd believed they were at the start of something that could be pretty damn amazing.

And then she ghosted him, which he'd taken personally. So, no, he wasn't playing a practical joke on her. He wasn't going near her.

"The crop circle isn't funny," she seethed as she rested the shotgun barrel on her shoulder and coughed. Thankfully, she seemed to think better of using it on him. Shotguns might not be the most accurate, but their spray was wide. He'd end up picking buckshot out of an arm or a leg in a best-case scenario.

"I wouldn't know," he quipped, not thrilled this was the first time they'd spoken in months—after what had been one of the best weekends of his life, as much as he hated to admit it now—and she had the nerve to accuse him of destroying her livelihood. "You're barking up the wrong tree, Brynne."

Should he call her out for cold-shouldering him for weeks now? Or was it months? No explanation. No 'kiss off' message. Just radio silence.

She had a lot of nerve showing up at his residence, threatening him. He'd chalk it up to being pranked, but none of this was funny. Besides, the look on her face said she meant business.

"Stay away from my land and stay away from me," she said through clenched teeth.

Travis had no idea what he'd said or done to rile Brynne up to this degree. It couldn't be his performance in bed. Could it?

No, not possible. He hadn't received any complaints so far in that department. It was probably his pride speaking, but Brynne seemed beyond happy when they were together in Austin. Ecstatic might be a better word. It had practically been a religious experience if anyone asked him. She hadn't spoken those words aloud, but a person knew when their partner was satisfied. They'd been so into each other he barely got dressed in time to meet food delivery drivers at the door. He just realized he'd cracked a smile just thinking about the time they'd shared.

What in hell's name had changed to make her want to shoot holes in him?

Travis put his hands up, palms out in the surrender position. "I don't blame you for being upset about your crops, but that doesn't give you a right to come blowing up to my home with a shotgun on your arm."

Free hand fisted on her side, she glared at him. "Do you swear?"

"I promise that I had nothing to do with whatever happened to your crops," he stated. "Do you want to tell me what this is about?"

She blew out a frustrated breath and he couldn't tell if she was relieved he wasn't the one responsible or even more upset that she had no clue who was responsible now. "I should go."

"Or you could come inside and explain yourself out of common courtesy," he countered.

"Common courtesy flew out the window the minute a skinned coyote turned up in the middle of the sadistic person's design," she got out through clenched teeth. Her face was flush despite cloudy skies and a cool breeze.

"Did you call the sheriff?" he asked. A tortured animal was nothing to mess around with, but he was even more disappointed—angry?—she could think so little of him. Anyone who hurt animals for sport should be strung up by their...*parts*.

"It turned out to be fake, Travis. But someone went to the trouble of pouring real blood all over it to make it believable."

"Damn," he conceded. "That's deranged."

"Exactly," she agreed, her body practically humming from pent-up anger. He could think of a good way to release all that tension, but not when she showed up believing he could have pulled a stunt like this.

"How could you think I would be responsible for such a—"

"I didn't even think of you as a possibility at first, Travis," she cut him off defensively. "Until I found this." She reached into her back pocket and produced a blue bandana with the Firebrand logo stamped in one corner.

"That's mine," he said to her, momentarily confused.

"I know," she admitted with a look that would freeze ice in Hades. "It's the reason I'm here and not at the sheriff's office. You have one chance to explain how this ended up on my property on the scene of a crime."

"Believe me when I say that I would tell you if I knew," he defended. "But thanks a whole helluva lot for the vote of confidence after…"

Travis stopped himself right there. Did he seriously have to point out the fact they'd made love? Don't even get him started on the time they'd spent together being the best weekend of his life to date.

He gave himself a mental headshake to stop his brain from tripping down that well-worn path again. He'd wasted enough time beating himself up over something he couldn't go back and fix. The question of whether or not he would do anything different if he could magically transport to that weekend was one he'd asked himself more than once after the snub.

Brynne's cheeks turned a darker shade of red. "The joke isn't funny, Travis. That's all I'm saying."

"Since I didn't prank you in the first place, I wouldn't expect it to be," he stated with a little more heat than intended.

"Fine then," she said with a loud harumph. "Guess it wasn't you."

He didn't want to state the obvious: that the prank could be on him, not her. Someone might be setting him up to look like the bad guy because of his mother's actions. It seemed half the town had changed toward him, keeping an eye on him like he might steal something at the feed store or crack if the gas station machine short-circuited while he was trying to make a payment now that one of his parents was in jail. They must not realize he wasn't close to his mother. The two barely spoke when they lived under the same roof. Now, she was locked up in Houston awaiting trial for attempted murder. The chasm between them had only grown.

Worst of all, his mother was guilty. She'd tried and failed to kill for greed so they wouldn't have to share an inheritance. How awful was that?

"Have you considered the idea someone might be playing the prank on me?" he asked, suddenly wondering if she'd ghosted him because she didn't want to be seen around town with a Firebrand.

Brynne stood there for a long moment. Her face morphed from confused to considering the idea to reality dawning on her. His family wasn't exactly looked at highly right now. She shook her head. "No, it never crossed my mind that someone might use me or my land to get back at you."

"No one saw us that weekend so—"

"Right. No." Suddenly, the toe of her boot became real interesting. "I didn't think anyone did, considering the fact we never left the room." More of those flames licked her cheeks, turning them a bright shade of red.

"You might want to set up cameras around your property if you think the bastard might return," he proposed, unsure why he felt the need to offer helpful advice when he should kick her off his land. Because he was a decent person, a small voice in the back of his head pointed out. It was the same voice that tried to convince him that his feelings for

Brynne were real and reciprocated that weekend. Clearly, the voice didn't know what it was talking about.

And then there was the fact he'd been dragged into this mess with the bandana. Now, he wanted to know who was behind the so-called prank, if it was one. Because it looked more like a threat.

"Guess I'll be heading out then," she said. Her eyes had the same look of a bull once it realized it had charged the wrong fence. He could swear he saw her nostrils flare even at this distance. "Sorry to have troubled you and wasted your time."

Instincts or maybe it was just habit had him wanting to tell her that her visit was no trouble at all. He'd be lying. She troubled him to no end. The question remained. What was he going to do about it?

~

BRYNNE STOPPED HER HAND MID-REACH, forcing it to move up toward her face to tuck a non-existent tuft of hair behind her ear. She couldn't remember when instinctively touching her belly had started, but the last thing she needed was to give Travis Firebrand the mental image of her cradling her stomach in any way.

Roaring up to his house was a bad idea, even though a piece of her wanted him to be responsible for the prank because then she would know it was meant to be harmless. And a growing part of her wanted to be able to tell him what else happened the weekend they'd spent together. Except the doctor warned her about spreading the news during the first trimester. Did telling the father count? She might turn Travis's life upside down and inside out in the way hers had been when she'd received the news. Pregnant.

What if the fetus wasn't viable like the doctor warned was possible? Then she would have put him through all this stress and worry for nothing.

Brynne was still trying to figure out how it had happened when they'd been careful. There was the time she feared the condom had slipped off in the heat of the moment but it had been her imagination working overtime and not reality. Right?

She clamped her mouth shut before she blurted out the news. Brynne couldn't be certain what made her want to vomit more: morning sickness or the bone-deep fear of becoming a single mother like hers had been. Brynne's mom had been younger, barely in her twenties, whereas Brynne's twenties were coming to an end. Still. The unplanned part—history repeating itself?—caused stomach bile to churn in her stomach and burn the back of her throat. The difficult life of barely making ends meet because Brynne's father said he was too young to handle the responsibility of a child. He'd bolted out of town two weeks after receiving the news and never returned.

Travis wouldn't disappear like her own father had. Travis had roots in Lone Star Pass. Travis was a decent human.

Still.

Panic tightened her chest, so she tried to release a slow breath only to realize Travis was studying her like a cheat sheet before a test. It didn't help calm her nerves any that he looked so damn good standing there. Travis had that whole tall, muscled, gorgeous look down pat. There was a long line of women who would cut their arm off to spend an evening alone with him. Or at least, there had been *before* his mother's arrest. Even now, she figured the line only shrank by a few. The only equal to fame was infamy.

TRAVIS: Firebrand Cowboys 9

"I should probably get going now," she stammered, figuring she better get out now before she blurted something out she might regret. Brynne was no good at lying or keeping secrets, especially not life-changing ones.

"You already said that," Travis pointed out, looking cool as a cucumber, despite his name being dragged into this mess with the bandana. It was common knowledge he wore the blue one. But that was one of his few predictable traits.

The weekend she'd spent with him had surprised her. He'd surprised her. Caught her off guard was more like it.

And she'd spent too many nights thinking about how amazing it had been to let go with Travis. To really let go and block out the outside world with all its stresses. Block out her mother's diagnosis. Block out the fact she was going to have to learn the farm business, from soup to nuts, in a matter of months instead of the years she thought she had with her mother being healthy. Block out the fact she'd just ended a relationship and hurt another person.

Her breakup with Ty Hudson had been a long time coming. They'd drifted apart months before, a year if she was being honest with herself. They barely spoke twice a week now that he'd taken on a second job as a driver in Houston after signing up to be available on an app. At one point, Brynne had been convinced Ty had been cheating, but he swore he wasn't. Ty believed, or so he said, their future was a lock and that he needed to save money for their future. He didn't have time for anyone or anything else in his life. What she'd found out after some digging around was that he had an online gambling addiction, which was the real reason for the second job.

The discovery had triggered her fear of instability and raised a huge red flag for her about having any kind of future together. She knew he needed help, but she couldn't help someone who lied to her. And he'd blown up at her when she brought up the subject at all.

Plus, to her thinking, they'd never spoken about a future together, not seriously. He'd hinted at one and she'd been quick to shoot him down. Dating had been fine early on. She didn't mind being exclusive. And she liked spending time with Ty when they were both free, which wasn't as often as he expected, considering she and her mother ran the farm together. They hired day workers during planting and harvest times. The rest was up to the two of them. The work was hard, but the farm meant everything to Brynne's mother. It had given her the independence to move away from her parents, who'd kept her under their thumb. They believed their daughter's pregnancy was some kind of punishment for sinning and didn't want to have much to do with a bastard child. The bastard child they were talking about was Brynne. Not a bastard, but a real human.

Glancing down at her stomach, she could never think of the little bean growing inside her as anything but a miracle. Granted, she'd planned to have her tubes tied the minute she could talk her doctor into the operation. But her doctor had said to wait until Brynne was thirty-five just in case she changed her mind. Since Brynne and her doctor, Lizzy Granger, had grown up together, Brynne yielded to her friend's advice.

She couldn't regret the little seed growing inside her even if her mother and grandparents agreed on one thing... Firebrands were bad news. The families' rivalry went way back long before Jackie Firebrand's arrest. Brynne was certain her mother had had bad dealings with the brothers Brodie and Keifer, although her mother refused to talk about what happened.

From what Brynne heard, those brothers thought they ran the town. They were competitive with each other to the point of destruction. They got what they wanted at any cost.

"It's just," she hemmed and hawed, not quite ready to leave since this was the only lead she'd had. "If it wasn't you, who was it?"

"I wish I had an answer for you. We'd both sleep better at night. Do you want a ride to the sheriff's office? We can talk to him together, see if he has any ideas," Travis reasoned. The look of betrayal on his face when she'd accused him would stay with her long after this conversation. She could admit to coming into the conversation hot. Her hormones were all over the place these days. They made mountains out of mole hills, and she'd be damned if she could stem her reactions, no matter how much she wanted to get a handle on them. This situation was very real, but accusing Travis could have been handled better.

"Teens get bored from time and time and pull stunts like this. Maybe he's getting other reports from the area," he continued.

She hoped the easy explanation was the right one. Her thoughts as to who was responsible hadn't panned out yet. Travis was innocent. So far, he had been her only suspect. He made a good point about the teenagers, though. Every few years it seemed a small group would get out of hand. Drinking and making bonfires out on private property or near the lake was one thing. There were times when they pushed the limits beyond painting spots on cattle or unscrewing the caps of ketchup bottles at the diner. They've replaced liquid soap with maple syrup in some of the public restrooms, which was annoying. Occasionally, a group had a bad seed and the pranks were darker. But that was rare.

Was this one of those times?

A little voice in the back of her mind picked this moment to urge her to do the right thing and tell him about the baby before she started showing or word somehow got out. He was the father, after all. Didn't he deserve to know?

Brynne hushed the voice. He was the *possible* father. Okay, that wasn't exactly what she meant. Travis was the father of a baby that was cooking, but it was more like a seed right now that *could* end up being a baby if all went well. Once again, what good would it do to get him all riled up for no reason if the seed didn't take? A baby wouldn't exactly be good news for him while his mother was about to go on trial.

Like Lizzy said, there was no reason to put the cart before the horse, so to speak. Once Brynne got the greenlight that the pregnancy was going to be a go full-term, she could deliver the news to Travis. At that point, she would be as close to one hundred percent certain they were having a baby as she could be. Anything could happen during a pregnancy, she realized. But getting past the first trimester was an important milestone, according to Lizzy.

So, Brynne would wait and basically torture herself with all her fears about whether or not she should keep the baby or consider giving him or her up for adoption. One thing was certain, though, she couldn't maintain the farm with an ailing mother and care for a newborn.

She sized Travis up. Would he even consider signing the paperwork to give his child away to a stranger if she decided on adoption? Hadn't he sworn off children as much as she had? He'd told her how much he'd rather be on the rodeo circuit than at the ranch working cattle. Did he resent having to stick around when his heart was somewhere else?

Of course, he would. He was human, despite looking like some sort of cowboy god with his chiseled features and intense blue eyes. Blue had always been her favorite color. His baby blues were a shade God himself hadn't figured out how to paint the sky with.

She could...*did*...get lost in them several times over the weekend they'd spent together. His shade of blue was her new favorite. It didn't hurt they were shielded by a matching set of thick, black lashes that only served to bring out their color even more.

When he stared at her or locked gazes, her resolve had a habit of flying out the window. Wasn't that wonderful? Travis had been a distraction—amazing as it had been—from life on the farm, which she loved, but the routine of it could become monotonous and lonely, especially since her mother's diagnosis.

News of her mother's disease had shaken Brynne to the core, especially as it came when it did. First, there'd been the breakup with Ty. It might have been long overdue but she hadn't been looking forward to it. Second, her mother's tremors became impossible to hide or ignore, along with muscles so stiff she couldn't open and close her hand like she was an NFL quarterback after a game. Third, it was becoming obvious her mother's bouts of confusion meant she couldn't handle all of her responsibilities on the farm. This wasn't like her mother's occasional bouts with depression during Brynne's youth. From her near-permanent position lying on the couch, she could answer questions. The brain fog now meant Brynne couldn't rely on answers.

The Parkinson's diagnosis had come before the weekend in Austin with Travis. Brynne had driven down to meet with a specialist. She'd gotten news no loved one wanted...the disease was progressive and going to get a whole lot worse. Fast.

"I'll drive," she finally said to Travis, shaking off her reverie. "Hop in the passenger seat if you're coming with me."

2

Despite the fact Travis didn't know Brynne well enough to understand her moods, he suspected more was going on with her than the crop circle. The use of real blood was alarming to be sure, but teens could be responsible. They sometimes took jokes too far. Not everyone was cut out for country life. Teenagers could become restless. Bored. With too much free time on their hands, they could get a little too creative. Teens weren't exactly known for making good judgment calls. Then there were the kids whose parents didn't look out for them, who ended up going down the troublemaker route. The sheriff might be able to clear this up during the visit to his office.

Living in Lone Star Pass suited Travis fine as long as he could be out on the land. Would he rather be strapped to a bull in an arena with a cheering crowd? Hell, yes. But that wasn't an option while he was needed at the ranch—a ranch that was as much part of him as taking risks in the bull-riding ring.

Travis climbed into the passenger seat of Brynne's truck and clicked on his seatbelt. This would qualify as a vintage model, considering the cracked bench seat and windows that were stuck just shy of being closed. He would offer to fix up her Chevy for her out of the goodness of his heart but realized that she might see his goodwill as an insult. The woman had an independent streak a mile long. Did he mention Brynne was also one of the most frustrating people he'd ever met?

A little air seeped through the crack between the window and the door, causing her thick, long, wheat-colored hair to whip around her face. She kept tucking tufts of it behind her ear, which seemed more habit than anything else. It wasn't exactly helping, but he decided this wasn't the time to point out the fact or recommend she throw her hair in a rubber band like he'd seen her do while working on the occasion times he'd passed by her farm.

To compliment those silky locks, Brynne had light brown eyes—eyes that looked like spun gold. There was a warm quality to them, even when she glared at him or shot daggers of ice. She was soft curves and sharp tongue, basically polar opposite vibes that confused the hell out of him. He'd heard rumors that her mother and either his father or uncle had had problems back in the day, but no one talked about what happened. His side of the family had bigger troubles than old squabbles at the moment. The other side of the family tree had moved on. All of his cousins had families of their own and seemed genuinely happy. Seven of his brothers had found true love. It was down to Travis and his brother Kellan to hang onto some semblance of single life. Travis had no intentions of getting married or having kids. His brother Kellan was about as likely to marry again as a wolf leaving her young while danger was present.

Due to recent events, Travis had spent enough time with

Sheriff Timothy Lawler to realize he would have questions about the scene that would lead to a trip to Brynne's home.

"On second thought, the sheriff will want to investigate the area and see the crop design for himself," Travis reasoned as he pulled out his cell phone. "I'll shoot him a quick text and ask him to meet us at your place."

"Does he have to?" she asked with a frustrated-sounding sigh.

What was up with the lack of enthusiasm?

"He's going to want to see for himself," he continued, wondering what she could be thinking that would make having the sheriff meet them at the site a questionable decision. "Because we can swing by and take our own pictures before hitting his office, if you'd prefer to do it that way, but I know he'll want to check out the area to gather evidence we might have missed."

Brynne white-knuckled the steering wheel. His curiosity grew. Why wouldn't she want a lawman on the scene of a crime?

"It's fine," she said after a thoughtful pause. "Everyone is going to find out eventually anyway."

"Find out about what?" he asked. The comment was loaded.

Brynne issued another heavy sigh. "The reason I was in Austin when we..." She flashed eyes at him before refocusing on the road and gripping the steering wheel even tighter. "Is because I was there to meet with a specialist."

"Is that why you hem-hawed around the question when I asked why you'd come to Austin?" he asked, but the question was rhetorical.

"Yes," she answered anyway. "That, and I didn't think where I went and what I did was anyone else's business."

The woman's independent streak was as long as US 83,

which ran from the Oklahoma state line to the Mexican border at Brownsville, an almost eleven-hour drive. He could admit it was probably one of the reasons her family's farm had done so well for so long. Brynne had a drive to succeed that caused her to dig her heels in when times were tough. At all cost?

"Are you alright?" he asked, hearing the concern in his own voice over the admission of Brynne meeting with a specialist. Was she seriously sick?

"Me? Yes," she reassured. "It's my mother."

"Right," he said. "You mentioned something about needing to check on something for her at the time, but you were evasive as to what that was and I didn't push you on it." This didn't seem like a good time to point out that they'd been in bed most of the time, preoccupied with the best sex of his life.

Damn. Was it?

If he was being honest, the answer was yes. It struck him as strange too because he wasn't the one-night-stand type. He might not be a long-term guy but he didn't hop into bed with just anyone. There needed to be something between him and the woman he was with that went beyond physical attraction for sex to be good.

"She has Parkinson's disease and it's progressing fast," Brynne stated. Reality slapped him in the face and his heart broke at the shakiness in her voice. "You know how small towns are with gossip."

He nodded his head but realized she hadn't taken her eyes off the road or lightened her grip on the steering wheel. "I think we both know that I do."

"Mom is proud," Brynne said. "She doesn't want word to get out yet, as she is still processing the news. So, I was hoping to avoid having the sheriff stop by. You know how it is around here. If someone visits your property, no matter the reason, it's impolite not to invite them inside, and then he'll for sure see how bad the tremors are. It'll invite questions Mom isn't ready to answer. I guess part of me wants to protect her for as long as I can, so that's the reason I don't want him at the farm."

"Understandable," he said. "And I'm truly sorry to hear about your mom." She might not have gone out of her way to be nice to Travis, but that didn't mean he wished a disease on her. He also realized how protective Brynne was of her mother. He respected their bond, even if he'd never experienced anything like it for himself. His own mother had been the 'sip champagne until she passed out' type. It wasn't until recently that he'd learned how awful her own childhood had been or understood the reason why she was so closed off. It didn't excuse attempted murder, but her background explained how she might have gotten to a desperate point.

Don't get him wrong, in no way, shape, or form did he condone her actions. Understanding how she was driven to hurt others because of her background was as far as he could get. He was still trying to wrap his mind around how his own mother could get to a place where taking a life seemed like the right play.

"Thank you," Brynne said, breaking through his reverie. Her voice cut through the noise in his head just like it had a couple of months ago.

"I can head the sheriff off, so your mother doesn't have to deal with him," Travis offered.

Brynne chewed on the inside of her lip. "Here's the thing, Travis. She isn't going to be thrilled if I bring you on her land either."

"What did I ever do to her?" he asked. The words rushed

out before he had a chance to think first. "Never mind. She probably hates me for the same reason half the town does."

"If it makes you feel any better, she's disliked your family my entire life," Brynne explained as gingerly as she could under the circumstances.

The comment shouldn't make him laugh the way it did. In fact, he laughed so hard he was pretty certain he snorted.

Brynne laughed too and the sound was musical.

∼

Brynne pulled over to the side of the road, idled the Chevy's engine, and then turned toward Travis, who was losing it. The man laughed so hard, it made her laugh too. And then her stomach muscles hurt from laughing so hard.

"It's been a long time since I found anything this funny," she admitted. "It's probably awful to admit that I forgot how to joke around."

Travis raked his fingers through that thick hair of his. "Life has been kicking my family in the teeth so hard, I forget up from down half the time. Finally, laughing feels damn good, if you ask me."

"Same here," she said on an exhale. "Laughing. Breathing. It's all good if you ask me. Why does adulting have to become so serious?" She wasn't kidding when she admitted to not laughing in far too long. Even Ty had teased her about being too 'buttoned-up' as he'd called it. He'd told her they were too young to be so stiff when, apparently, he wasn't being serious enough. His gambling had been for fun, at first. At some point, she had no idea when, it had become a habit that led to addiction.

She might not be 'fun' according to his earlier version, but at least she hadn't fallen down any of the rabbit holes of addiction. He'd been the same way with drinking too, whereas she could take it or leave it. An occasional glass of wine with a hot bath was exactly what she needed after a hard day. But then the hard days started racking up and there weren't enough baths to fix her, and she hadn't let that one glass of wine become a crutch.

Rolling up her sleeves and chipping away at a problem until she found a solution was the only way she'd ever resolved anything. To do that, she needed a clear mind. Did that make her monotonous?

"Am I boring?" she asked Travis, figuring she had nothing to lose with the question. On second thought, maybe some of her pride was at stake.

Travis laughed harder, so she gave him a playful tap on the shoulder. Her hand met a steel wall. The man had muscles stacked on top of muscle.

She made a dramatic show of withdrawing her hand and shaking out her fingers. "Ouch."

"I'd offer to kiss it and make it better, but I'm afraid you'll deck me so hard you'll knock out a tooth or break my nose," he said through waves of laughter.

"Alright, funny guy," she shot back. "I'm surprised you strung together that many words through your snorting."

He threw his head back and laughed. "You heard that, huh?"

"It was impossible not to," she quipped through rolls of laughter. Honestly, this was the first time she'd relaxed in longer than she could remember, aside from that weekend with Travis.

In the moment, it had been the best thing that had ever happened to her. After, she couldn't believe she'd let her guard down when she had an uphill battle ahead of her with her mother's health. Plus, Travis had his own battles to fight with his mother. But she couldn't bring herself to call their time together a mistake.

Travis finally slowed his breathing back to a normal pace. "You do realize nothing we said was all that funny."

"Nope, it wasn't," she admitted, but cracked a smile anyway. She leaned her head against the headrest. "Do you remember being a kid?"

"Bits and pieces," he said.

"All I wanted to do when I grew up was make art," she revealed. Had she ever spoken those words out loud to another soul? No. Not even her mother, whom she loved dearly.

"Makes sense from what I knew of you in school," he said. She was surprised by his response.

She took in a fortifying breath, feeling lighter than she had in too long. "I wanted to go to art school in Dallas and make my mark on the scene."

"Why didn't you?" he inquired.

"Mom's bouts with depression got worse as I got closer to leaving home." Brynne surprised herself by continuing to open up rather than shut down like she normally did. "I decided Dallas was too far and realized Mom wouldn't be able to manage the farm on her own, so I told myself I'd make art in my free time." She paused. "Little did I know at the time there would be no free time. I came home every weekend to work the farm just to keep things going."

"And now?" he asked. "You've been out of school for a while."

"Doesn't seem like I have," she said. "When did life spin so far out of control?"

"Good question," he agreed, before sitting up straight again. A signal to get back on track? Was this getting too personal?

Brynne still felt bad about not returning Travis's texts. The weekend they'd spent together had confused her. Reset her clock, actually. She'd never felt so at ease with anyone before, not Ty, nor anyone she'd dated before him. She'd never had better sex with anyone in her life. She wasn't the kind of person who could throw caution to the wind when it came to sex or investing in a relationship. She had to get to know someone first.

Technically, she'd known Travis on some level most of their lives. They grew up in the same town and knew of each other. She had more fun than she wanted to admit teasing him while they were in high school. He'd been a freshman when she was a junior.

"After graduation, life got serious for me fast," she said to him, not quite ready to get back on the road. "Adult life quickly followed. My mother moved in and out of depression over the next few years, so I took on more responsibility around the farm while at community college to keep food on the table and the place running so there would be a crop year after year. Something had to give so I quit school."

"That's a lot of responsibility for a young person," Travis said.

"You would know better than anyone," she stated. "Weren't you working the ranch for your grandfather from the time you could walk?"

His laugh was tight this time. "You could say that."

"I thought you wanted to go on the rodeo circuit," she said.

"That was a pipe dream," he admitted. "The ranch needs me, so I stayed."

"I guess we both have that in common," she realized.

"What's that?"

"We ended up doing something out of obligation instead

of following our hearts," she admitted. It was a sobering reality.

"Would you?"

"What?" she asked.

"Do something different if you could?" he continued. His tone took on a new level of seriousness. More like introspection.

"Yeah, I think so," she said, almost confused by the simple question. "I guess I never gave myself permission to think like that. I mean, what would it accomplish? Nothing would change, right? I'd still be doing what I do because I could never leave my mom alone."

"You don't think it's important for us to at least ask ourselves what we would do if we weren't bound by duty?"

She shrugged. "I have my mom to think about. Me working the farm is how I give back for the childhood she gave me. Besides, what else would she do if not this? She told me that she doesn't have any skills outside of the farm, which she'd figured out through hard knocks."

"Didn't her parents help out?"

"No," she said, shaking her head. "Not after she brought a bastard into the world. They essentially disowned her and by the time they realized they'd made a mistake, she was too hurt to let them back into her life. She'd worked for the previous owners of the farm for free, learning the business. They were older and not ready to move. They let her buy the place from them, making payments directly to them. Once she figured out how to survive and couldn't go back."

"What about you? Do you have a relationship with them?" he questioned.

"Why would I?" she quipped, a little faster and harsher than intended, and then sighed. "What I mean to say is that I didn't know them from Adam, so they're strangers to me. I was nothing but a bastard child to them. I didn't lose anything like my mom did. Does that make sense?"

He nodded. "A whole lot."

That was the dangerous thing about Travis Firebrand. He was easy to talk to. He almost made her believe life would work out and that she could want things. Things like her mother turning out to be fine. Things like a real relationship. Things like a future with choices.

"What about you?" she asked, turning the tables.

"We should probably go," he said, a muscle in his jaw ticked. "We don't want the sheriff to show up at your house before we do."

Way to redirect the conversation when he was in the spotlight. Had she overshared? Overstepped her bounds? Offended him in some way?

Maybe he was right. The sheriff might have answers or at least be able to point them in the right direction. And there wasn't much point in trying to squeeze answers out of Travis. He wasn't able to answer the questions she asked of him, so how could he answer the unspoken ones?

3

"Alright," Brynne said, clearly put off by Travis's rapid end to their conversation. He wasn't trying to be a jerk, but they needed to get back on the road. Getting personal would only lead to him being burned again.

Freshman year in science class was the first time Travis worked with a Bunsen Burner. The experiment was supposed to demonstrate how different liquids affect the way paper burns using flame-resistant paper. He remembered the tongs, the glass beakers, and cutting several small pieces of paper. There was ethanol and water, if memory served. The experiment was supposed to end with the paper not igniting. But Travis had leaned over too far and burned the back of his hand with the flame.

The only thing he'd learned from the experiment was not to touch the flame on a Bunsen Burner twice. Well, that and the fact he wasn't going to work in a lab as a career choice. He could skip that section on career day at school. Then again, he'd always dreamed of becoming a bull rider.

The rest of the ride over was spent in silence. After riling

Brynne up, Travis knew better than to poke the bear by asking questions or trying to reignite the conversation. A piece of him regretted the move, but keeping a safe distance was in both of their best interests, whether they wanted to admit it or not. The voice in the back of his mind tried to put up an argument to say this time would be different, but he squelched it before the darn thing could gain any traction.

"Will your mother be okay with me being on her land?" he asked. "Under normal circumstances, I'd say she needed to get over herself since I'm there to help, but I'd rather not upset her with everything else she's going through." He didn't want to make this any harder on Brynne either, if he was being honest

"She'll have to get over it, won't she?" Brynne's voice could freeze boiling water on contact.

"I guess so." Travis made a mental note to tread lightly. Her mood was more intense than he'd seen in the past. The playfulness—if it could be called that, considering how sexy she was—was gone from her eyes. Worse yet, she didn't make eye contact after she parked.

His thoughts shifted to her going into defensive mode when it came to her mom. Not to mention what they were about to face inside the crop circle.

What he knew, so far, was some jerk had ruined part of Brynne's crop by cutting a design in her field. This must have happened overnight, last night. Then, there was the skinned coyote that was a fake. Real blood had been thrown around. Where did the blood come from? Animal? Person?

The hair on the back of his neck stood up. A warning.

Folks who started out killing animals were the ones who fixated on death. If left unchecked, the fixation would only grow. Was a serial killer testing the waters? He'd watched a show about them once, focusing on the notorious killer in

Milwaukee who targeted young men, drugged them, and then committed horrific acts before killing and eating or preserving some of their body parts. This criminal had started killing animals at a young age, fascinated with death.

Making a crop circle didn't fit in with the crime, unless it was meant to be some type of symbol.

"Did you manage an aerial view of the crops?" he asked Brynne as she sat there, staring out the windshield. Her and her mother's home looked like something from a storybook. The two-story had white paint with black shudders and a wraparound porch. There was a pair of white rocking chairs on the front porch, along with ferns and plants both hanging and in planters. The wood floors on the porch were painted steel gray. He took note of the fact there were only two rockers along with a small table in between. He imagined Brynne and her mother sitting out there, watching the sun set while sipping tea or having a glass of something stronger.

Was it strange there was only room for two? Shouldn't there be space for visitors? Brynne was young and her mother wasn't exactly old. Before he could finish the thought, the driver's side door slammed shut. Didn't that move jolt him out of his internal thoughts?

He exited on the passenger side.

"No," she admitted, in case you're listening this time. Had he zoned out? "I don't have a working drone."

He glanced around. The crop circle wasn't immediately visible. "How did you discover it?"

She pointed to the sky where vultures circled. "Them."

Vultures weren't exactly uncommon in these parts and critters died from natural causes as well as ending up as prey in the food chain. "Was there a reason you decided to investigate immediately?"

"My favorite barn cat has gone missing," she admitted. "I feared the worst and didn't want to leave her out there, to be picked at by those gross oversized birds."

He would have done the same. He gave a nod.

"We can go look for her now if you want to," he offered a second too late since the sheriff pulled onto the drive. "Or would it be best if I knocked on the door and introduced myself to your mom?"

"She's met you before, Travis."

"Not properly," he corrected.

"That might be true, but she does know who you are, so I think we're good." Brynne stood there for a long moment, tapping her toe. "Unless, of course, it's important to you in some way."

"No," he blew it off. Wanting to meet her mother as an adult so she would like him better shouldn't matter to him. But since his mother's arrest, those things got under his skin a whole lot more. "I doubt it would change her opinion of me anyway."

Sheriff Lawler pulled up next to them in his marked SUV, parked, and then exited as the screen door opened and Ms. Beauden stepped onto the porch. She craned her neck to get a good look around at who was on her property. Even from this distance, Travis could see her frown when her gaze landed on him.

"Go back inside, Mother," Brynne instructed, but her tone was soft as silk. "I've got this, okay?"

"Well..." Ms. Beauden looked confused. "I guess. If you say so. How about I make some iced tea for our guests."

He took note of the fact she didn't leave the porch to come any closer. Politeness warred with her need for privacy, and the whole episode played out on her face.

"That's fine, Mom," Brynne said. "We can take ours on

the porch. Just set the tray down and get back to your computer entries. I know how busy you are this time of day."

"Alright," Ms. Beauden said, resigned. She disappeared into the picture-perfect home.

The fact they kept the place ship-shape and ran the business on their own was impressive. He was only one small piece in the Firebrand Cattle machine, and it took everyone to keep business rolling. Cattle might be different than corn, but there were plenty of Firebrands to pitch in, whereas this operation was run by a party of two with summer hands for harvest because you need the corn combine harvester with a truck to drive alongside it.

Being able to run a successful business alongside her mother was one of the reasons he respected Brynne so much. He'd also had a crush on her since freshman year despite her need to tease him beyond belief. Two years might not be much of an age difference now, but it could have been ten years for how wide the maturity gap had been at fifteen and seventeen.

Brynne had come across as so mature to him, and sophisticated. He'd felt like nothing more than a pimple-nosed kid compared to her. His voice still squeaked back then. He'd been what the pediatrician had called a late bloomer. Considering the fact all his cousins and brothers were well over six-feet-tall and had had their height from an early age, Travis had felt like the shorty of the family aside from his cousin Brax. He'd secretly feared his height would never come and he'd be stuck craning his neck when he spoke to his brothers.

Of course, all that was a big exaggeration. But then teenagers weren't exactly known for being calm and mature. Some might have been. But the majority were a bunch of insecure kids trying to outgrow childhood into adults. The road was bumpy as hell for most.

"Sheriff Lawler, I'd like to thank you for stopping by," Brynne started as she stuck out her hand.

The sheriff took the offering and then turned to Travis for the same greeting. Unlike most ranchers or ranching families, Lawler was about as fair-skinned as they came. His ginger hair was cut military short. His hawk-like nose gave him an air of authority. His light brown eyes, full of compassion, helped earn the trust of those he came across in the line of duty and as well as on a personal level. He wore jeans, boots, and a tan shirt with the word Sheriff embroidered on the right front pocket, which seemed standard issue when it came to law enforcement working in small towns.

"Fill me in on what you found, when you found it, and who you think might be responsible," he said to Brynne after the perfunctory greetings.

∽

"It's probably best if I show you as we talk," Brynne said to the sheriff. Being back on the farm caused the tiny hairs on the back of her neck to prickle. The feeling someone was watching tightened a knot in her stomach.

Brynne glanced around, searching for unexpected movement. Decided her imagination was working overtime.

Showing up at Travis's home without warning with a hothead full of accusations had turned out to be a better idea than she realized. His presence had a calming effect on her, which was probably good for the baby. Plus, if this little bean stayed put and grew into a big bean, it was probably good for the seed to hear Travis's voice and to know it calmed their mother. Brynne had no idea what that might be like for a kid. She'd never experienced it, considering she had no memories of a father. Her grandfather's voice only caused her mother to tense more, and the sound of it became fingernails on a chalkboard to Brynne after she found out that voice had said the word *bastard* when referring to her.

She'd learned early on in life what it was not to be wanted. Which was exactly the reason she would make her own child feel welcomed into the world, even if circumstances might force her to give it to another couple. That would only happen if she was one hundred percent certain they would be the best possible fit for her child.

Was she seriously considering adoption? A voice in the back of her mind pointed out she didn't have a choice. She had to consider all options.

Walking along the path toward the scene of the crime, she noted how the sheriff stopped to examine stalks, the ground, and generally took in everything in their surroundings. It was good for an investigation but scared her on a personal level. A guy who was paid to notice things might not be the best person to have around while she was trying to hide what might end up a whole person in her belly.

There wasn't much she could do about blocking his powers of observation. She needed his help to find and put an end to whoever did this. Because this could be a warning and, if so, what did this person intend to do next?

"Have you had any similar calls, Sheriff?" she asked as they approached the manmade clearing.

Sheriff Lawler shook his head. "This is the first, and I hope the last."

"Does that mean someone is specifically targeting my mother and I?" she asked as a cold chill raced up her spine.

"It's too early to make any assumptions," he said, calm as anyone pleased while her blood pressure was on the rise. Taking in a couple of breaths meant to calm her only ushered in the smell of death. The acrid smell of blood filled the air as a breeze whistled through the leafy stalks. It was late in the season for most crops but corn outlasted the others, sticking around until late October or early November in these parts. Harvesting was in full bloom at the moment as silos were being filled.

"How do you and your mother harvest all these crops?" Sheriff Lawler asked.

"We hire day laborers," she admitted. Out of the corner of her eye, she saw Travis tense up at the admission. Why? Plenty of folks picked up day labor in town. She didn't run a big enough business year-round to hire full-time. He wouldn't know that considering he was part owner in one of the most successful cattle ranching businesses in Texas, if not the country. His grandfather, the Marshal as most had called him, built a small empire. His public face in the community garnered a heap of praise, but her mother wasn't fooled by the man. She didn't have such a high opinion of Marshal Firebrand like so many of the others. Half the town believed the man walked on water.

For a long time, she'd borrowed her mother's dislike for the family. Except the Marshal's grandchildren had been nothing but nice to her in school. She might not have been friends with any of them on a personal level, but they held doors open and acted with good manners. They couldn't have been too bad with all that courtesy ingrained in them. Then again, people had secrets. She would have never guessed his mother was capable of trying to take someone's life.

Travis, despite being two years younger than her, had

been the one to catch her eye. She'd teased him almost mercilessly. He seemed to take it all in stride, firing back on occasion. She'd nicknamed him Freshy during her junior year. He'd been shorter than his brothers and cousins but soon shot up. His face matured his sophomore year and then her cheeks turned red when she teased him.

It had caught her off guard. Luckily, she was a senior. Grades didn't mix a whole lot. Sure, there was the occasional senior who dated a junior, but most stuck to their own grade when it came to going out socially.

A wave of nausea like she'd never known bent her forward as a wind gust blasted her with more of the acrid scent.

Travis was by her side in a heartbeat. "Are you alright?"

"I'm fine," she said quickly. Too quickly?

Bile burned the back of her throat as her chest seemed to catch on fire. Great, she could add heartburn to the list of discomforts. A growing part of her wished she could leave town for the next six or seven months until the kid was born. She could think a whole lot clearer if she wasn't a bucket of overwrought hormones. Under the best of circumstances—as in already married before a pregnancy—dealing with the changes happening in her body would be hard.

Before she could continue down that unproductive road of wishful thinking, the first dry heave hit. There were a few others but thankfully, nothing came back up. She'd take whatever small miracle she could get.

As she stood up, she realized her hand had gone to her stomach. Biting back a curse, she tucked it inside the back pocket of her jeans. It was then she realized Travis stood there, studying her with questions in his eyes.

Not now. Please don't let him figure out what was going on with her now.

"Did you see the fake coyote was skinned?" she asked the sheriff as those icy fingers took hold of her spine, refusing to let go. What if someone had targeted her? What if one of her workers held a grudge against her? Was threatening her? Or plain old trying to scare her?

To what end?

The mind was an interesting thing. The minute someone put an idea in there, it came up with all kinds of support for it.

"We hire family men who need the seasonal work to put food in the mouths of their families," she finally defended. "Several come back every year. They look out for us and wouldn't let us hire someone questionable."

"I'll need a list of names," Sheriff Lawler said. "If you have records."

"We're a legitimate business, Sheriff," she said. "But I take folks' word for who they are, and we pay in cash as they request, because not everyone has a bank account. That a problem?"

"Shouldn't be," Sheriff Lawler said. "Will your workers be here tomorrow?"

"I pick them up at five-thirty in the morning," she stated. "You're welcome to come with me tomorrow."

"I'd like to be there too," Travis piped in.

Really? Because being around him longer than absolutely necessary was a huge risk, especially with the way he just looked at her belly.

4

"Is that a good idea?" Brynne practically stammered in response.

"My name is involved because of the bandana," he motioned toward the material hanging out of her back pocket. "I have every intention of getting to the bottom of what's happening here and who is behind this."

Sheriff Lawler turned his attention toward Travis. "What bandana?"

Travis gave the sheriff the quick and dirty lowdown in a matter of a couple of minutes. "You know what my family has been...*is still* going through right now. I'm guessing someone might believe we're easy targets or wants to drag our family name through the mud a little more than it already has been."

The sheriff shook his head in disgust. "I'd like to believe the good folks of Lone Star Pass are above this kind of nonsense, but recent events have proved the opposite." He made a sour face. "I barely recognize half the town right now."

Travis would second that, except he'd grown up under

the watchful eyes of that half of the town. It seemed they'd been waiting for the opportunity to say *I told you so* when it came to the Firebrands on his side of the family being bad. Like it confirmed what they'd believed all along, despite the fact Travis had been a decent student in school. He'd played sports to the best of his ability. He might not have been as successful as some on the other side of the family, the 'good' side, but he was honest and hard-working and that should count for something.

The town turned a blind eye when it came to his good qualities. If he heard hints about apples not falling far from the tree one more time, he'd...

Travis realized he was clenching his fists. Since that line of thinking was about as productive as squeezing a wrench to get lemonade, he shifted his thoughts to the investigation. "Wasn't there something going on with the Walton twins recently?" he asked the sheriff. "Weren't they getting into some kind of trouble?"

The sheriff nodded. "Wrong kind, though. Junior stole a tire from the tire store because he didn't want to admit to flattening his by hitting a curb too hard while fiddling with his phone to change his music."

"Theft isn't the same as damaging someone's property," Travis agreed. "And there's no one else you can think of who would think a prank like this was funny?"

"Not off hand," Sheriff Lawler admitted. "The Taylor boys have a wild streak, but they've been much quieter this year with college applications and football. I haven't run them off anyone's property since summer for organizing a bonfire or figuring out how to get alcohol for a party."

"This doesn't seem up their alley either," Travis agreed.

"Which leaves us with a disgruntled worker," Sheriff Lawler reasoned. His logic made sense when Travis really thought about it. Wouldn't it be someone close to Brynne's inner circle?

"This feels personal," Brynne stated as though she was coming around to the idea someone she hired could have it out for her for whatever reason.

"Revenge is a possibility," Sheriff Lawler pointed out. "Which could be aimed at either household."

The way Brynne's gaze dropped to the ground, Travis couldn't help wonder if she believed the prank was most likely aimed at him.

"Let's assume for a moment that this is about revenge against the Firebrand name," Travis said, leaning into the idea for a minute. "Why target me? I haven't done anything to anyone. I haven't hurt anyone that I know of." He didn't go down the path of his own ego taking a hit when Brynne didn't answer his texts. That was another story altogether. Had someone linked the two of them together in Austin?

Nah, he reasoned there was no way anyone from Lone Star Pass had seen them. Had Brynne told anyone about their fling? Would she do that? And who? Her mother was her best friend, but she couldn't stand him. Brynne would poke her own eyes out before telling her mother about the fling with a Firebrand. Young people didn't generally stick around Lone Star Pass unless they were inheriting a family business or had to stay and work to keep one going. Usually, when someone graduated high school, they left to get a job or go to college. Austin wasn't too far away, so a few ended up there. Some stayed in touch with folks back home for a while. Travis didn't do social media even though he'd signed up on a dating app once when he realized Lone Star Pass was dry as a desert. He'd dated the few single women who'd interested him. Became uninterested just as fast.

Other than the dating app, he didn't do social media

accounts. It seemed like a bunch of hype, and he was looking for someone real. Plus, he liked the idea of seeing someone in person, hearing their voice before asking them on a date. Chemistry was more than just good looks, and he'd never been able to gauge whether or not he had chemistry with someone on a computer screen.

"Good question," Sheriff Lawler said after a thoughtful pause. "At this point, we're looking at trespassing and damaging property, both misdemeanors."

"This feels like a threat," Brynne interjected.

The sheriff listened but didn't respond. Was he thinking in a different direction?

Travis motioned toward the damage. "What would someone have to gain by doing this?"

"Good question," Sheriff Lawler said. "And if it's a threat, why?"

They stood there for a long moment but no one came up with an immediate reason.

"Halloween is at the end of the month," Travis pointed out as the realization hit him.

"True," Brynne stated.

"Which could mean this is the first of many to come," Sheriff Lawler said, shaking his head.

It could be the tip of the iceberg.

"I'll get the drone out of the back of my vehicle so we can get in the air," Sheriff Lawler said. "If this is some sort of symbol in the crops, we might get a better sense of what we might be dealing with from an aerial view."

"I need to take a break from this smell," Brynne stated, pinching her nose. Her skin had paled and she looked like she might be ready for round two of dry heaves or worse.

Granted, it didn't smell like a rose garden but there

wasn't enough blood to fill the air so much he couldn't breathe.

"I'll wait here," he said, wanting a few minutes alone with the site to do his own investigating.

"Before we take off on our own for a few minutes, what about relationships?" Sheriff Lawler asked, pointing the question to Brynne. "Are you seeing anyone or have you recently ended one?"

"Yes," Brynne said after clearing her throat. Her gaze dropped again and the toe of her boot became very interesting.

Travis's stomach sank and his chest fisted. How would it look to the sheriff if Brynne was honest about their fling and then how she'd ghosted him? Even Brynne believed Travis was responsible. He was, in fact, her first thought. The sheriff would think along the same lines and Travis would have to explain, no prove his innocence before the lawman would seriously consider another suspect.

The sheriff stood there, expectant. "Well? I need a name."

Once again, Brynne cleared her throat. It seemed to be her go-to move when she didn't want to deliver news she didn't think would go over well.

Travis's trapeze muscles tightened like overstretched strings on a cello. He steadied himself for the flood of questions that were about to follow.

"Ty Hudson," she finally said. Her brown eyes flitted up toward Travis and, for a split second, he thought her cheeks turned a couple shades of red. "But we broke up a couple of months ago. He would have no reason to pull something like this now."

"Has he been in contact with you recently?" Sheriff Lawler asked as Travis did his level best not to react to the name. The breakup with her boyfriend would have timed nicely with the weekend she'd spend with Travis in Austin. Was that the reason for their fling? Because her heart had been broken and she was looking for an easy rebound?

Brynne didn't strike him as the type to use someone, but recent events had taught him that you never truly know someone else. He never would have expected his own mother to attempt murder for financial gain.

Was that the reason Brynne hadn't returned his calls? He had just been 'move on' sex to her, when she'd rocked his world that weekend? When he thought about it like that, he should probably be offended. He couldn't regret the best sex of his life because it had shown him that he needed to raise the bar on the women he spent time around. No one came close to making him think about the possibility of a future together before Brynne.

Damn that she hadn't felt the same when he'd been so sure of himself that weekend. He'd been on top of the world thinking the most beautiful and intelligent woman on the planet belonged to him. He'd conjured up a fantasy about the weekend being the beginning of something that was about to blow his mind. Had he seen 'forever' with Brynne? One weekend wasn't enough to predict the future with anyone, but it was the first time he'd believed in the possibility of one.

Life had kicked Travis in the teeth on the home front. He'd most likely been reaching for some kind of stability and hadn't found *the one* that weekend. Whatever that meant.

Travis had no idea who Ty Hudson was, so he shouldn't be jealous.

"Did Mr. Hudson break up with you or was it the other

way around?" Sheriff Lawler asked the question on the tip of Travis's tongue.

Travis tried not to give the impression that he was hanging on by the edge of his seat, waiting for her to answer.

But he was.

～

"I BROKE UP WITH HIM." Talking about Ty in front of Travis felt like the worst kind of betrayal. Brynne risked a glance at Travis and was met with a stone-cold expression. Was he angry at her for having a boyfriend before the two of them spent the weekend together? If she told him about the pregnancy now, would he question whether or not he was the father?

The overwhelming urge to blurt out that she and Ty hadn't had sex during the last six months of their relationship rose. There'd been no sleepovers. No quickies. No longies, whatever that meant. In fact, the deeper he fell into his gambling addiction, the less time they spent together period. Call her old-fashioned, but she couldn't get in the mood when everything about their relationship felt off. She believed the two of them should be in counseling to figure out what was happening with them, not between the sheets. Sex never solved problems between couples. Unsatisfying sex was often an indication of where the relationship was headed. She'd learned that lesson from Ty.

So, there was no chance the baby was Ty's. There'd been no fighting sex, no makeup sex, and no sex any other time.

"Was Mr. Hudson upset?" Sheriff Lawler continued.

"Yes," she admitted. "Again, it happened a while ago so I don't see how he would be showing up now for revenge. Wouldn't Ty have done that a couple of months ago?"

"Most likely, yes," Sheriff Lawler admitted. "Unless he's fallen into hard times or something happened that reminded him of the relationship that he lost." The sheriff's gaze shifted to a spot behind her right ear. "I've seen something as simple as someone scanning for TV shows on Netflix be the cause of remembering they'd been hurt by someone they loved and being the catalyst for them to do something destructive. Normally, though, the person reaches out first and then experiences another rejection they see as the final straw. Has Mr. Hudson been in contact with you lately, Ms. Beauden?"

"He had, probably still has, a gambling addiction. I called him out on it, asking him to get help. He refused and told me I was making up an excuse to break up. Still, I'm probably the last person he wants to see. Right?"

"Not necessarily," the sheriff said. "It would be odd if he didn't try to reach you first."

"I blocked his calls after the first week of our breakup. And even though I don't post very often on social media, I blocked him there just in case."

Which meant she had no idea if he'd tried to reach her and that could have upset him enough to pull something like this, according to the sheriff. Ty also could have been a pot of water sitting on a burner, stewing and heating up to boiling point.

Brynne just couldn't see Ty going to all this trouble. In the last few months of what had become of their relationship, they rarely saw each other. But then folks weren't always predictable. She was one hundred percent certain her mother would never have been in a relationship with Brynne's father if she realized he would walk out when the going got tough.

Speaking of fathers, she needed to circle back with Lizzy

to find out the exact date the pregnancy was in the clear so she could inform Travis. If he was going to be a deadbeat, she needed to seriously consider adoption. There wasn't enough money left over to hire a babysitter, and Brynne couldn't imagine working the farm while packing a newborn around. Didn't women usually sit out of work for six weeks while their bodies adjusted and they got used to being mothers? There was no way she could pull off keeping the farm afloat, taking care of her mother, and taking care of a newborn. To say her plate was full was an understatement.

"Sounds like you really have no idea if Mr. Hudson has been attempting to reach you," Sheriff Lawler said.

"Wouldn't he stop by my house if he was truly being persistent and needed to talk to me to find out where I stood?" she questioned. "Why do this when he hadn't bothered to talk to me to see if he had a chance at a comeback?"

"Those are good points," Sheriff Lawler said. "Still, I'll need his contact information, home and work addresses. I can send a deputy to Houston to interview Mr. Hudson tonight. If you have an idea where he'll be, that would be a huge help."

"I can tell you where he worked the last time I saw him just over two months ago, but he's taking on working as a car service to random passengers to bring in more money that was supposed to help build a future together," she said as the first signs of Travis's irritation started to show. He tapped the toe of his boot on the ground and she'd caught him clenching his jaw a couple of times. He hadn't made much eye contact since the subject of her ex came up. As much as he didn't strike her as the jealous type, he must have questions as to the timing of the breakup. No one wanted to feel like a rebound person.

Travis Firebrand had been anything but.

Brynne had nothing to offer beyond a weekend. Her focus had to be on learning the rest of the farm business since she'd always divided the chores with her mother and getting her mother the best care possible as her body literally turned against her.

It occurred to her the sheriff might ask for Travis's phone records in order to cross him off the suspect list.

That wouldn't exactly paint Travis in a good light. Under normal circumstances, his texts would look like someone who didn't understand why she'd abruptly stopped talking to them after a great weekend together.

But these weren't normal circumstances, and the texts could be twisted around to make it seem like he had it out for her. Especially when she took his mother's situation into account.

The evidence might all be circumstantial, but folks could be quick to judge and even faster to condemn. All anyone had to do was look to the internet to find proof. Someone might be caught out of context having a mental breakdown. All another person had to do was record a snippet and then put any frame they wanted around it and people could go ballistic with mean comments. Cancel culture was real. And she would add 'quick to condemn without the facts' to that list as well.

"Okay," Sheriff Lawler said. "I'll go ahead and grab the drone now while you look up the information."

Travis opened his mouth to speak. Brynne's heart dropped.

5

"Hold on, Sheriff," Brynne said before adding, "I'll go with you."

Before Travis could get his question out, Brynne disappeared down the path along with the sheriff. Would the fact she hadn't told Lawler about the weekend they'd spent together come back to bite him in the backside?

The way his luck had been going, it was highly likely. The fact should be the biggest thought on his mind. Was it?

Nope.

His brain kept looping back to the fact Brynne had just broken up with her boyfriend when he'd spent the weekend with her. For now, he forced himself to focus on the crop markings despite the loop of questions circling around in his mind. The drone should be able to get high enough to depict any kind of symbol that might be present. A symbol could have a meaning behind it, like a warning. The next thought he had was whether or not her ex had decided to scare her. If it was this Ty Hudson person, how did he get ahold of one of Travis's bandanas? Had the man been spying on Brynne that weekend? Did he know about the two of them? Holy hell, it could be a possibility. Brynne's Chevy was distinct. It wouldn't be hard to spot.

Why wait until now to threaten or scare her? Did he think enough time had passed that she might miss him?

The sheriff made a good point about an ex trying to make contact and then facing a final rejection before making a move like this one. When Travis thought about it in those terms, a disgruntled worker could make more sense. Anyone who lived or worked in Lone Star Pass could end up with one of his bandanas. The Marshal had given them out like candy on Halloween to trick-or-treaters when he'd been alive. Said it was good for the ranch and for business. Free advertising. Blue had been Travis's favorite color, not deep blue but light blue like the sky in spring after a rain shower.

And then there was the episode with Brynne almost vomiting. Her face had lost all color. There wasn't enough concentration of smell to be the culprit. He didn't want to feel bad for her for all the stress she must be under trying to figure out how to run a farm on her own while helping her mother adjust to the bad health news. It was a lot for anyone to have on their plate. Was that the reason she didn't call him back or return his texts? Her plate was too full?

Wasn't that just an excuse for not being into him?

She hadn't blocked his number on her phone. He got voicemail on the few times he'd called. Was that a good sign? At least he hadn't been dumped in the same bucket as Ty Hudson.

Travis moved around the circle, refocusing on the facts of the investigation as best he could, while something he couldn't quite pinpoint niggled at the back of his mind.

The fake coyote wasn't exactly a fake animal. It had to

have come from the taxidermist's office. Travis wondered if there'd been any reported thefts or break-ins at Jefferson Cutler's place. He was the only game in town or for miles around. So, the coyote had to have come from his office unless there was a hobbyist out there Travis hadn't heard about.

Then there was the blood. Could the barn cat have been sacrificed? Her blood scattered around? Or was this chicken blood? Hell, it could have come from Firebrand livestock or anywhere else for that matter.

Could it be human?

Travis pulled out his cell phone and performed a quick search to see if a lab could determine whether the blood was human or animal. The answer came quickly. They could.

Right. The barn cat. But then she'd also believed it might have died or been killed because of the vultures. He made a mental note to ask for a description of the missing cat and he hoped like hell the blood didn't belong to the innocent animal.

As his mind started running around in another unproductive circle about Brynne and her ex, his hands fisted. He heard Ms. Beauden's voice carried by the wind. Her tone should be fingernails on a chalkboard after finding out how much she couldn't stand him, but he was determined to change her mind. Being lumped into the category of 'one of those Firebrands' without deserving it wasn't something he could tolerate. If she got to know him and still disliked him, he could live with that.

"Tea is ready," she shouted as he forced a smile.

Since it was still hot despite being late October, he figured a pitstop for a refreshment couldn't hurt. Besides, he often had the best success solving a problem when he walked away from it and distracted himself. The method had gotten him through pre-calculus in high school and still worked to this day.

Plus, he was curious about how Brynne's mother would react to him face-to-face and, if he was being completely honest, find out if she hated him specifically or just the Firebrand name. The first would be next to impossible to overcome, no matter how much he tried to convince her that he was a good person. If she didn't like Firebrands in general, he might have a shot to change her mind about him personally.

Brynne and the sheriff were already on the porch by the time he cleared the field. He cut across the lawn and took the steps two at a time onto the porch. The look on Ms. Beauden's face when he approached wasn't a real good sign about how this was going to go.

"Isn't this a surprise," the older woman said, wrinkling her nose in a move that made him want to lift his shirt and sniff his armpits to see if he stunk. Given her recent devastating medical news, he would give her a wide berth.

Ms. Beauden was thin and fiddled with her hands as she practically glared at him. He couldn't help but wonder if there was a story behind those judgmental eyes involving either his father or his uncle. Or both. "This is the most company we've had in days."

Brynne picked up a glass of tea as her face twisted. "What do you mean in days? The workers never visit the house, Mom. What company have you had that I don't know about?" Travis had spotted an outhouse well behind the home tucked away in the tree line the workers probably used if they needed to relieve themselves. So, there was no practical need for them to enter the main house.

Her mother's face puckered up like a dried grape. The

words *cold shoulder* came to mind after the way she looked at him. "Nothing. Never mind." She wagged an accusing finger at Travis. He took note of how shaky her hand was. "What are you doing here?" She turned to her daughter. "You know how I feel about Firebrands, Brynne."

Was that part of the reason Brynne had walked away from him? She didn't want to betray her mother by becoming involved with the enemy.

Why did the thought sting so much? He should be used to 'holier than thou' types in Lone Star Pass by now.

"He's my guest, Mom," Brynne said as her cheeks flamed with what looked like mortification. She turned to Travis, "Please excuse my mom. She hasn't been feeling well or she wouldn't forget her manners and be so rude to one of my guests." She turned to her mother with a warning look. "Right, Mom?"

Ms. Beauden shrugged a shoulder.

"Wouldn't you feel better if you went inside to lie down, Mom?" Brynne suggested.

"I'm fine right here," Ms. Beauden retorted, clearly put off.

"Thank you for tolerating me, Ms. Beauden," Travis said, clueing into what she'd said a minute ago.

The shoulder raised but she didn't look over at him. Instead, she stiffened. Since she wasn't having the same reaction to the sheriff, Travis figured it wasn't all men she couldn't stand the sight of, and he'd been right about her hating Firebrands.

"You mentioned having company," he continued. "Has anyone else stopped by in the past few days?"

"Ty was here, but Brynne knows..."

Ms. Beauden's voice trailed off as her eyes widened to the point of saucers.

Brynne's gaze became laser-focused. "What did you just say, Mother?"

Ms. Beauden made another face. "Well, it's no secret the man is still in love with you. So, yes, he came over to check on me."

"What did you say to him?" Fire shot from Brynne's gaze.

"He was upset," her mother continued. "What do you expect? I told him that you'd come around in time."

"You should never speak for me," Brynne stated, folding her arms over her chest. "Ever. And especially not to an ex-boyfriend."

"He was worked up about something," her mother defended. "What was I supposed to do?"

Travis looked at Ms. Beauden. *Really* looked at her. She looked scared. Granted, her defenses were up but under the surface it was easy to see she was frightened. Bags underneath her eyes told him she most likely wasn't sleeping at night. Folks didn't make their best decisions when they were sleep deprived. Cattle ranchers were a rare breed who'd trained themselves to go without sleep for days on end during calving season. They eventually caught up on rest. Plus, they were young, as the older ranch hands liked to remind them. Normal folks rarely trained themselves to function while sleep-deprived.

Brynne shifted in her seat, turning toward the sheriff. "I'll have the information you requested about Ty in your hand before you leave this property."

Ms. Beauden shot a look at Travis that could best be described as a warning to stay away from her daughter. The older woman might not ever like or respect him, but that wouldn't stop him from protecting Brynne. If Ms. Beauden knew the circumstances, she would most likely welcome help. Then again, based on the way she was tearing him apart with her gaze, maybe not.

"You," Ms. Beauden said under her breath like an accusation.

Travis had a feeling this wasn't over.

∾

Brynne could hardly believe Ty had stopped by the ranch and her own mother hadn't seen fit to tell her about the visit. This was rich. "Is there anything else you aren't telling me, Mother?"

"What would I have to hide?" her mom asked. She looked like a five-year-old, who'd just been scolded on the playground for being too rough while on the monkey bars. This was real life, *Brynne's* life. Her mom needed to take a step back.

"Clearly more than I realized," Brynne said as her mom bristled. She'd always been close with her mom. They'd promised a long time ago not to keep secrets. It had always been the two of them against the world. The diagnosis was creating stress fractures in their relationship. Was it causing her mom to spin out mentally and emotionally?

Brynne reminded herself to take it easy on her mom. She wasn't herself lately for obvious reasons and could go into one of her funks at any time. Brynne was thankful the diagnosis hadn't completely spun her mother into depression, which didn't mean it wouldn't. She softened her tone when she said, "So, please answer the question. Is there anyone else you've been talking to behind my back?"

"No, sweetheart," Ms. Beauden said, shrinking in her seat. "I wasn't trying to hurt you."

Brynne believed her mom was being honest. She

couldn't remember a time when her mom purposely hurt Brynne. All those times she'd checked out, unable to get out of bed, had inadvertently hurt. But those didn't count. Depression was hard on everyone, especially the sufferer. Brynne didn't fault her mom for the times she struggled with it.

The way her mom had just treated Travis was inexcusable, though. She would circle back to apologize on her mom's behalf. He didn't deserve to be spoken to like a dog because of his family's actions. Speaking of which, Brynne had never pushed her mom for an explanation as to why she hated the Firebrands so fiercely. Maybe it was time to find out. Brynne might not be able to change the past or her mother's mind, but she could stick up for an innocent person. Travis had done nothing to deserve the treatment he was receiving.

"Would you like iced tea?" Brynne said to Travis, realizing her mother hadn't asked.

"No, thank you," Travis responded.

For a split second, an image of her, Travis, and their baby together on this porch with her mom smiling flashed in her mind. Brynne was dumbfounded. She'd never wanted marriage, let alone a child. What was different now?

Nothing, she reassured. Her mother would never welcome a Firebrand into her home. Brynne stopped right there. The baby was a Firebrand. If the fetus was viable and Brynne decided to keep him or her, wouldn't her mother have to love a Firebrand?

She'd been so dead set against the family that it was impossible to see a time when she would change her mind. And it wasn't like her mom was a jerk. She was the kind of person who baked cookies for seasonal workers in the shapes of leaves and decorated them for fall.

Most of all, when her mom could get out of bed and wasn't debilitated by depression, she had been at every school function and parent-teacher conference. She did her part to run the farm and managed to put a decent meal on the table every night. She packed lunches for Brynne and braided her hair. In short, she'd been a good mother who didn't deserve the hand fate had dealt.

Brynne could pitch in more when her mother was depressed. She could step up to take appointments and hire seasonal workers. But she couldn't erase her mother's hatred for Firebrands and might never understand why.

The fact she'd kept this secret from her mom had been wearing on her. Again, what if all the worry ended up being for nothing? Although, she had enough morning sickness to make her believe she had a strong pregnancy going on. Sickness that was showing no signs of easing up. That had to mean something.

She glanced up to find Travis studying her again. Questions danced in his eyes, and they were questions she had no answers to. She pulled out her cell phone and hit her contacts. She found Ty's. "Here you go, Sheriff."

Brynne shared the contact information. The sheriff excused himself almost immediately. He was most likely arranging for a deputy to drive to Houston, so she sent a text with Ty's job information and the car service he worked for. She reminded the sheriff of the gambling problem, not to get him into trouble, but he might believe the deputy was showing up for that if he was innocent of the crop crime.

The sheriff picked up the drone, disappeared into the field, and then the hum of the engine filled the air.

"Ms. Beauden, I'd like to thank you for your hospitality," Travis started. Brynne knew exactly where he was going with this...an exit.

"I don't see your vehicle, Mr. Firebrand," Brynne's mom said, craning her neck to check the parking pad in case she was wrong.

"Your daughter was good enough to pick me up to bring me here," he supplied.

"Why would she do that, and what is Sheriff Lawler doing here?" her mom asked. "I forgot to ask in all the 'excitement.'"

"Don't worry about it, Mom," Brynne said quickly. "You already have enough on your mind."

She should probably warn her mother about the possibility a seasonal laborer could be upset with them, except it didn't ring true. What reason would anyone have to be mad at someone who baked cookies and made sure workers always had fresh water?

"Seems like maybe I should be concerned," her mother responded as her gaze moved from Brynne to Travis and back.

"I can assure you there's no need to get worked up," Brynne stated as Travis stood.

He excused himself next and then made a beeline for the field.

Brynne turned to her mom. "It's not okay with me how you just treated Travis."

Her mom tried to wave it off like she was swatting a fly.

"No, Mom." She wasn't getting away with it so easily. "What has he specifically ever done to you in order to cause you to lose all manners?"

"Well, I guess nothing," her mom replied. "But he has Firebrand blood coursing through his veins, and you'd do well to remember the fact."

"That's not a reason to be rude to someone you don't know," Brynne pointed out.

Her mom exhaled. "What is it really, sweetheart?" Her shoulders relaxed a little now. Did she really hate Firebrands so much? Because that could cause a problem later. "Tell me what's troubling you."

An entire list of troubles came to mind. But the most troubling was the one where she and Travis became a family.

Brynne's mom moved to the rocking chair and reached over to touch her arm. "I know you've been dealt a horrible blow too."

Her biggest fear so far had been her mother figuring out the pregnancy. Had she? Mothers had a way of finding things out in surprising ways. Mother's intuition was a real thing. When her mother was clear of depression, hers worked double time.

"Yeah," Brynne hedged as panic caused her heart to fist in her chest.

"This awful diagnosis has us both stressed to the gills," her mom continued. "Don't think I haven't noticed how sick you've become. I know it's my fault."

Relief was quickly replaced with sadness.

"Oh, Mom," Brynne said. "You shouldn't worry about me right now. I can handle it."

"I've seen it, sweetheart," her mom continued. "You haven't been yourself in weeks. It's the reason I agreed to let him drive up for a visit. I thought maybe you'd feel better if you had someone to talk to."

"Who? Ty?" Brynne asked, not hiding her surprise. Her mother didn't know Brynne as well as she thought if she believed Ty would reduce her stress in some way.

"You two were close at one time," her mom said, unfazed.

"That was a long time ago," Brynne said.

"You can't blame a mother for wanting to know her daughter will be okay once she…"

"Don't talk like that, Mom," Brynne said, wiping a rogue tear from her eye. "You're doing fine right now."

"We have to face what's happening," her mom reminded her, with that awful blank look on her face. It was the way she always looked right before slipping into the darkness where she couldn't get out of bed for days, let alone shower.

"Mom, I need you to stay with me," Brynne urged. "If you can. Please. Stay alert so we can figure out a plan for you to get better."

Her mother didn't respond, she just smiled as warm a smile as she could muster and nodded. The darkness beckoned and Brynne had never felt so helpless to stop her mother from sliding into it.

6

"The images from the drone's camera will show up here on my cell phone," Sheriff Lawler said to Travis as he navigated the controller. "If I can get reception, that is."

"I should use a satellite phone while out on the land in remote areas, especially when I'm by myself but I don't," Travis admitted. "There's something nice about being unavailable in a world that tries to make folks available twenty-four-seven."

"You probably should at least bring the phone in case you need to call for an emergency," Sheriff Lawler pointed out. "But that's the lawman in me talking. Before I took this job, I used to disappear one day a month just to find a new fishing hole. Cell phone off. No way to reach me." His voice was wistful. "That was a long time ago and a longwinded way of saying I understand the need to disappear." The sheriff didn't shift his gaze from the drone. "I'm hoping one of those times you need to disappear wasn't in the last twenty-four hours."

"Are you telling me that I'm a suspect?" Travis asked,

knowing he would end up on the list since his bandana was found on the scene.

"Not at this point, no," Sheriff Lawler said without so much as a glance at Travis. "Your family has been through a lot over the past few months. There's no denying you deserve a break. All I'm saying is that I'm bound to do my job to the best of my ability and, to tell the truth, I'm hoping it doesn't lead me down the trail of a Firebrand."

"No one hopes the same more than me," Travis agreed. "It crossed my mind someone might be trying to set me up, though. Which would mean you would have to investigate me as part of your job." Was this the time to tell the sheriff about the fling with Brynne? It might only be a matter of time before the trail led to him anyway. How would it look if the sheriff was surprised by the information after spending time together right here at the scene? It wouldn't exactly point to Travis's innocence. "Since you might have to go down that road, there's something you should know."

Sheriff Lawler didn't blink. The man had probably heard everything before in the course of his job. So, this might not come as a surprise.

"A couple of months back, Brynne and I ended up at the same place at the same time in Austin," Travis explained. He would leave out the part about knowing why Brynne was there, because it wasn't his story to tell. Brynne and her mother could decide when the time was right to tell the sheriff about Ms. Beauden's disease. He couldn't imagine losing his ability to control his muscles a little bit at a time. He'd checked on his phone what the future looked like for Ms. Beauden and it was part of the reason he could shake off her cold-shouldering him before. "We ended up spending a weekend together."

"Oh?"

"That's right," Travis admitted. Coming clean wasn't easy and he hoped Brynne wouldn't hate him for telling the sheriff. But Travis was convinced it was the right thing to do. "I'm willing to turn over my phone if you'd like to take a look."

"What will I find on it?" Sheriff Lawler asked.

"Not much more than me texting her a few times after and there were a handful of phone calls, texts, and voicemails," he said. "One I'm not so proud of, because I'd had a few before making the call." Travis wasn't a big drinker but he'd been stewing on more than just the rejection from Brynne that night. His better judgment had taken the night off, causing him to keep the beers coming when he should have stopped. "I left a message that, looking back, I wish I hadn't."

"You said this happened a couple of months ago?" Sheriff Lawler asked.

"That's right," Travis agreed.

"And you haven't had contact since?" Sheriff Lawler continued as his eyebrows drew together.

"No, sir," Travis said. "Normally, I wouldn't think twice about any of this, but in light of what happened here last night, I thought you should have all the facts."

"Did Brynne Beauden show up at your place to pick you up or accuse you?" Sheriff Lawler asked. That man didn't miss a trick.

"To accuse me," Travis admitted. It sounded bad when he heard the words spoken out loud. It sounded bad for him in particular. "And, you know how you asked if I got lost yesterday?"

"Yep," Sheriff Lawler admitted, breaking formality.

"I didn't but there's no way for me to prove it," Travis continued. "So, I fully understand if you need to put my name on the other list, even though I hate the thought."

"You might have been the person being targeted in this crime," Sheriff Lawler pointed out. "And most guilty folks didn't volunteer information like this in my experience."

"You're still welcome to my phone," Travis said, appreciating the fact Lawler didn't seem immediately ready to hang Travis by his boots with the least bit of ammunition.

"I'll take you up on that because, like I already said, I dot every i and cross every t during an investigation," the sheriff said after a thoughtful pause. "Plus, if your name comes up again, it'll be easy for me to shoot down since I will have already checked your phone."

"I appreciate your confidence in me, Sheriff," Travis admitted. "I don't get the benefit of the doubt around town much anymore."

"It's a shame some folks decide to judge a whole family by the actions of one or two folks," Sheriff Lawler said. "I've always known you to be honest, Travis. And in my county, folks are innocent until proven guilty."

"You won't find any evidence against me," Travis said, tensing before adding, "not anything that's not circumstantial because I've done nothing wrong." He realized how defensive he was coming across. Forcing some of the tension in his shoulders to relax, he continued, "Your support means the world, though."

"Good folks deserve a fighting chance," Sheriff Lawler said.

"What do I need to do to give permission for you to search my phone record?" Travis asked. If he'd just pointed the finger at himself, so be it. Better to go ahead and get this out of the way now before the bastard responsible had a chance to up his game and make Travis look even guiltier if that was the game being played. Sometimes, the best defense was a good offense.

"I can take a look now and then you can swing by my office to sign a consent form for me to have access to your phone records," Sheriff Lawler supplied. "Volunteering the information like this will go a long way toward proving your innocence, should it come to that."

The fact Travis felt the need to have this conversation at all was more disappointing than anything else. He was frustrated with his town and with all the folks in it.

Was it time to pack it in? Hit the circuit before he aged out? Because the piece of him that wanted to dig his heels in and prove everyone wrong was losing ground.

"Alright," he said. "I'll stop by later today."

"If I'm out, you can get the form at the desk," Sheriff Lawler said. "No need to wait on me."

"Sounds good," Travis said. He made a mental note to take care of that first thing as he dug inside his pocket for his cell. He stood there, patiently, as the sheriff finished snapping images from the drone.

Travis had no idea how the sheriff would interpret the messages, but he had a feeling he was about to find out.

∽

BRYNNE STUDIED HER MOTHER, decided she was hiding something. Had she upset one of the workers? Her remark would have had to be nasty to elicit this kind of response. Plus, Brynne believed she had a sixth sense about folks. She never brought anyone to the ranch, one of her dependable seasonal workers wouldn't personally vouch for. It wasn't just good business because she ended up with the best workers, it was a safety precaution. Two women living alone on a farm could be an easy mark.

She knew differently. They had a house alarm and

Brynne could defend herself against anyone in a fair fight. She knew how to shoot and kept a shotgun within reach. It wasn't living paranoid. It was living smart. It was living realistic. When most folks in Lone Star Pass left keys in their vehicles and their doors unlocked, she did the opposite. She'd learned a long time ago that just because she didn't expect something to happen didn't mean it wouldn't.

Brynne didn't take chances.

Which was why she felt the need to ask her mother the question outright. "Are you telling me everything, Mom?"

No answer.

"Mom?"

Her mom made a show of buttoning up her mouth and making an 'I'm innocent' gesture. It was the reason Brynne knew her mother was up to something.

"Don't you trust me to take care of you and the farm?" she asked, not hiding her hurt.

"It's not about you, sweetheart."

"What was that supposed to mean?" Brynne asked. "Because I'm fully capable of running this place." Brynne continued digging for information and hoping to hit the jackpot. "I've been doing fine so far." She didn't know how to handle the books and don't even get her started on working with the accountant during tax time. Her mother's headaches increased tenfold during tax season. "I still have a lot to learn before I'm running everything on my own."

"What about all the stuff you have to do for me?" her mom said.

"Are you concerned that I'll drop the ball?" Brynne wondered what her mom believed happened when her episodes got bad. Even as a young child, Brynne had taken care of her mother when the darkness took over and she couldn't help herself.

"No, nothing like that," her mom said without conviction. "I just think you have a lot going on and could use help. That's where I thought Ty could come in, and it's the only reason I entertained his calls."

"Did you reach out to him first?" A betrayal like that would crack an already strained relationship with her mom. Strained because life was hard, and Brynne was doing the best she could to help her mother adjust to the devastating news while holding it together herself. Brynne had no time to worry about herself, and bottling up her feelings made them leak out at the most inopportune times. Like the other day while working in the barn. She couldn't find the little tabby and suddenly it felt like the walls were coming down around her. She plopped down on a hay bail and cried for twenty minutes.

But it was the thought of anything happening to the tabby that caused the waterworks to start. Why hadn't she cried one single time since finding out about her mother's diagnosis? She'd been so mad she could barely see straight. She'd felt so much pity for her mom that she wished she could cry. But no tears came. Only anger and frustration. Brynne wanted to smack a wall or run until her legs gave out.

"No," her mom said scornfully, pulling Brynne back into their conversation and out of her heavy thoughts. "I wouldn't go behind your back like that." She sat up straight, prim and proper-like. "When he called and asked to stop by, I wasn't sure how you'd feel about it. I thought you should hear what he had to say, but he showed up at the wrong time. You had gone into town. Don't think I haven't noticed you've been spending a lot of time away. Is it because of him?" She motioned toward the cornfield.

"I'd prefer if you stayed out of this one, Mom," Brynne

said, softening her tone. The last thing she wanted was for her mom to sink into another dark hole. Even back in school, she'd done everything in her power not to give her mother a reason to go dark. Her grades were good. She'd worked hard for them and earned every A. She'd earned every B too, because some subjects kicked her backside. Math, for one. The thought of taking over the books of the farm was enough to give her nightmares. But, you know what? She'd figured out how to pass math in school. She'd figured out how to hire good workers and cook for both her and her mom from a young age.

Brynne could figure out accounting too. It might take time and was a far cry from the art she craved to create instead, but her mom wasn't going anywhere for what Brynne hoped would be a long time. Even if Mom couldn't do the work, she could advise Brynne on what to do. As long as she stayed lucid and didn't give into the darkness. Brynne's worst fear was that her mom would just check out mentally from the stress one of these days and not come back.

"I wasn't poking around, if that's what you're insinuating." Her mom had become testy and defensive in the past few weeks. Her mood change was understandable, though, given the circumstances. She needed time to process.

"All I'm telling you is that I'm good with my personal life," Brynne felt the need to say.

Her mom practically clamped her mouth shut to keep from spitting something out. What?

"I've known you my whole life, Mom," Brynne started. "What are you not telling me?"

"I have no reason to lie to you, sweetheart," her mother said, changing tone as fast as the weather changed in a Texas winter.

"Withholding information when being asked is a form of lying," Brynne pointed out. She had no plans to get up from this chair until her mother came clean. Did it have to do with Ty coming for a visit? "What are you up to?"

"Nothing, like I said." Mom's face did that pucker-thing again like when she was deeply offended. "How long have you been seeing that Firebrand boy?"

"He's not a boy, Mom."

"How long?"

"We aren't 'seeing' each other." Brynne made air quotes with her fingers when she said the word, *seeing*.

"Why is he here?" Mom set her iced tea down and crossed her arms over her chest. "Why did you think it was a good idea to bring him onto my land?"

"*Your* land?" Brynne asked defensively. "I thought this was *our* home."

"I didn't mean it like that," Mom said.

It was taking pretty much everything inside of Brynne not to blow up at her mom and demand answers. Of course, it would only strain their relationship further, and losing her temper might release a little pressure in the moment but she would feel awful about it later.

She'd learned speaking in anger was never worth it in the long run. The temporary pleasure always came back to bite her. So, she took in a slow breath. The pregnancy hormones weren't helping matters. She exhaled a long, slow breath.

"You keep accusing me of lying and keeping secrets, but I'm not the only one in this house who isn't spilling her guts," Mom finally said.

Panic gripped Brynne. "What's that supposed to mean?"

"You won't be able to care for it all alone," Mom said before issuing a pregnant pause and looking at Brynne like she'd looked right through her daughter and now everything. Those words sent an icy chill up her arms.

"Care for what, Mom?"

"You know very well what I'm talking about," her mom scolded.

Brynne could barely breathe. Did her mother know about the baby?

7

"These darn cell phones," Sheriff Lawler said, drone in one hand and his cell in the other. "They never seem to work when you really need 'em."

"The images aren't coming through," Travis said out loud what he already knew. "Coverage is spotty in these parts, but I'm preaching to the choir with that statement."

Sheriff Lawler nodded.

"I have what I came for, so I best be heading out," the sheriff explained. "Stop by my office, sign the consent, and I'll take an official look at your phone."

"As soon as Brynne takes me back home, I'll head over."

"Sounds like a plan." The sheriff gestured toward his full hands in apology for not offering a handshake. "See you in a few."

"Will do, Sheriff."

Travis had already scanned the scene long enough to know there wasn't anything else out here for him to discover. He wished he could bring the barn cat to Brynne and ease at least one of her concerns. The dark circles cradling her eyes said she wasn't getting much in the way of sleep. This situation wasn't helping.

As he walked away from the scene, he couldn't help but wonder if someone out there hated him enough to plant his bandana here. To what end? He'd asked himself this question before and was asking it now.

Did someone know about the fling he'd had with Brynne? Or was that guilt talking over the fact they'd hid it from everyone?

If so, why wait until now to act? A couple of months had passed. Why wait this long for...what? Revenge? To link the two of them together? To 'bust' them for a fling? They were both grown adults capable of doing whatever they pleased as long as it didn't hurt anyone else.

The lone thought that came to mind was Brynne's ex. Had her mother somehow found out about the fling and then told Ty when he visited recently? Or was it the other way around? Brynne's mother had seemed genuinely caught off guard by Travis's presence. Then again, it might have been Ty who told Ms. Beauden.

Travis could let those thoughts run circles in his brain and never figure it out. So, he forced those thoughts aside and readied himself to face Brynne's mother. Her approval shouldn't make a hill of beans difference to him. But it did.

Normally, he couldn't care less who liked or disliked him. It was one of the reasons he loved working the land so much. Nature didn't care who you were. A lightning bolt didn't discriminate. It would strike him just as fast as it would strike the town's preacher. It didn't separate people into 'good' and 'bad' categories. It just struck. Nature was the great equalizer.

He broke the stalk line and saw Brynne engaged in what

looked like an intense conversation with her mother. *Great timing, Firebrand.*

Since Brynne was his ride and he couldn't exactly walk home, he sucked in a breath, put on his big boy pants, and turned toward the porch.

The second Brynne saw him coming, she stood up and made a hand gesture that looked like she was ending an argument. *Done* was the connotation. This should be fun to interrupt.

Before he got the chance, Brynne hopped off the porch, not bothering to take the stairs, and met him halfway across the lawn. She was in a huff, gripping her Chevy keys like the world would explode if she dropped them.

He knew better than to ask questions, especially when she grunted one word as she passed by him. "*Chevy.*"

Travis turned tail and headed toward the passenger side. He stopped short of opening the door. Brynne, however, claimed the driver's seat, put on her seatbelt, and revved the engine.

"Are you getting in?" Brynne finally asked.

"What do you think about switching seats?"

Travis readied himself for the fight that was sure to come.

"No one drives my truck but me," she insisted, gripping the wheel tighter. "I promise to calm down if you get in. My mother is watching our every move right now, and I can feel her eyes boring through my skin."

How could Travis turn down an invitation like that? Easy. Like this. "Tempting, but I like to show up to places in one piece, if you don't mind."

"I'm sorry," she said, releasing a breath that sounded like she'd been holding in the entire march across the lawn. Her shoulders relaxed and so did her grip on the wheel. She rolled her shoulders a couple of times and he could almost see stress melting off her body. She turned toward him and conjured up a warm smile. The kind that made her gold-spun eyes glow. "Better?"

He nodded and opened the door before sliding onto the seat and buckling up. "I have no idea how you can go from a hundred back to zero so fast when it comes to stress."

"Years of practice," she said without any fanfare. It wasn't a joke or meant to be ironic. It was just fact. She backed out of the parking spot and then headed down the drive. "My mom has struggled with depression in the past, so I got used to being able to turn off my emotions so I didn't push her too far."

"What happened if you did?" he asked.

"I would lose her for days, weeks, sometimes months," she said with raw honesty. "So, I developed an off switch before it got too bad."

"You and your mother have always been close," he surmised. "It must have been hard being just the two of you."

"It's all I've ever known," she admitted. "I wouldn't know any different."

"A big family can be a real pain in the rear end," he said with enough enthusiasm they both laughed. "I mean that in the literal sense. Eight brothers and nine cousins, all guys, meant a whole lot of wrestling and arguments. But I know what you mean about having a mother you had to tiptoe around at times." He paused, thinking of the similarities and the differences in their situations. "In our house, that was all the time. There were no good days."

"You never gave the impression of being close with your parents," she said. "Anytime I saw you together, you were always very formal with them."

"Yes, ma'am," he said. "No, sir."

Granted, it was the way of the South. But his home was probably more formal than most. There was no warmth to soften the edges of being so formal all the time. It was like wearing a tuxedo day and night. Uncomfortable, but you knew what was expected. You also knew you'd sweat most of the time it was on.

"We didn't do that in my house but I think I was more like a companion and, sometimes, a caregiver with mine," she said. "There were times when I wished I had a mother more than a friend but life could have been worse."

"Ever think it could have been better?" he asked.

"Of course, I did," she defended. He wasn't trying to get under her skin with the comment.

"I overheard someone say that once," he stated. "It got me thinking. I wasn't trying to offend you. Apologies if I did."

Brynne seemed lost in thought for a few moments. Then, she nodded. "It makes a lot of sense actually. It's so easy to pass everything off with the other comment when, maybe, we should expect life to get better." She shook her head. "I'm getting too philosophical here."

"My fault," he argued. "There are times when I'm out on the land by myself for days, and the strangest thoughts hit me. Or I'll remember some random thing I overheard and then overthink it to death."

"I always liked that about you, Travis," she said, surprising him with the comment. "Even back in school, you were always thinking. I could tell. There was always a lot going on inside your mind. I used to wish I could peel back the layers and see what had you so preoccupied all the time."

"I'm sure it wasn't as profound as I would have liked it to

have been able to admit right now," he said with a smile. Compliments had never gone over easy for him. They normally downright embarrassed him. From her, they were easier to take. Why? He had no idea.

"You've always been smart, Travis."

"Tell that to Mrs. Hightower," he disagreed.

"She couldn't teach high school geometry, so hardly any of us could pass it," she defended.

He could get used to her coming to his defense. Then again, wouldn't she just hurt his ego again if he gave her room? It would be easy to like Brynne more than he wanted to admit after she'd ghosted him. It would be easy to lean into the attraction.

But a relationship between the two of them could never go anywhere. She'd been clear about that when she turned her back on him. Even if she changed her mind right now, there was no going back for Travis despite the hollow feeling in his chest at the thought of not seeing her again.

Stepping away would be for the best for both of them.

∼

TRAVIS WAS TOO HARD on himself. "You should give yourself some credit. You're one of the smartest people I know."

He shot her a look that said, other than one weekend, they hadn't spent enough time in the same room for her to make that statement with authority. He would never believe her because he didn't realize the crush she'd had in high school or how she'd always paid attention when he spoke.

Pulling up to his home, she said, "I'm sorry that I accused you of playing the dirty prank." Maybe it had been wishful thinking on her part. If Travis was responsible, she knew the prank would end there. It hadn't occurred to her that someone might be trying to get back at him, her, or both.

Then there was her mom to consider. What had she said to Ty? Could she have said something that upset him to the point he would do such a thing? Could she have mentioned the pregnancy?

Should she pick up the phone and give him a call to do some damage control? Find out what he knew?

Her mom had Brynne scared she'd figured out the pregnancy. She couldn't have. Right? Brynne had been so careful. She drove to a rest stop to take the test so there would be no evidence lying around. The last thing she needed was for her mother to find a pregnancy test in the trash, positive or negative.

"Don't worry about it," Travis said as he reached for the handle, no doubt to escape her company as quickly as possible. His voice had an I'm-used-to-it-by-now tone that caused her chest to squeeze. In the heat of the moment, it hadn't occurred to her how offensive it might be to be accused. It also hadn't occurred to her that he could be set up. Who would pull a jerk move like that?

"You have my number if you need to reach me," she offered.

"Yeah, no, it doesn't seem like you blocked me," he quipped. The words were followed by a brief look of apology.

"Fair point." She could take her lumps if it meant he might forgive her. Would he, though? And she wasn't talking about ghosting him. She was talking about the pregnancy. Would he resent her for the rest of his life?

Could she ask in a different way? Needle around until she figured out what his reaction would be?

"You said you'd rather be on the rodeo circuit than working cattle before," she started.

"That's right," he said, leaning into the opened passenger window. "What about it?"

"Do you resent not being able to? Go on the road, I mean."

"At times," he said without hesitation.

Well, she'd tested the waters. They were boiling. She got burned. At least she knew what she was dealing with and that she'd made the right decision in holding off on telling him about the bean. If there was even the slightest possibility of the pregnancy not taking, there was no need to stress him out. And it would stress him out. A baby strapped a person down more than a job.

If he didn't want anything to do with the child and she decided to keep it, Brynne had no idea how she would handle her mother, the farm, and a newborn.

But that was future Brynne's problem. Today's Brynne had enough to contend with. No need to stockpile problems that she wasn't facing this red-hot minute.

Travis cocked his head to one side. "Why do you ask?"

"No reason," she stammered. "Just curious." She added those last couple of words in the hope it would somehow explain everything.

He wasn't buying it.

"This isn't the best question right now, I get that," he started. "But is everything okay?"

What should she tell him? *No, it's not because I'm pregnant with a possibly viable fetus and you're the father. Meanwhile, my home life is crumbling. Literally crumbling. And I have no idea how I'm going to make it through this week, let alone the next or the rest of this year.*

"It's this thing with my mom," she settled on. "We've been at odds ever since the diagnosis. She just keeps giving up and I get so frustrated." She flashed eyes at him. "You know?"

He didn't. How could he?

"If it makes you feel any better, my relationship with my mother has always been strained," he admitted. "Even though this is just more proof that I have no idea who she is, I can't shake the feeling I've failed her in some way."

"It's not your fault, Travis."

"Your mother's situation isn't yours either," he countered. "Does hearing that make any of it feel any better?"

"No," she said. It didn't. "Have you gone to see her? In Houston?"

He shook his head. "A few of my brothers have visited her, but I haven't been able to figure out how to cope with seeing my own mother in jail."

"It might help with some of the guilt," she offered. "If you feel bad, it might mean that you need to do something."

"On that, we agree," he said. "I just don't know what that is. Believe me, if I believed seeing her behind bars would somehow make this all okay, I'd be there tomorrow."

"I know you would," she said.

"You keep saying things like that, Brynne," he said, catching her gaze and holding onto it. "But you don't know me as well as you think you do."

What was she supposed to do with that statement? Risk stressing him out over the possibility of becoming a father? Make him hate her for the rest of their lives as if he didn't already resent her?

She should have returned his texts or calls or both. She couldn't. Not when life was spinning out of control. She had her reasons. Would they be good enough for him?

8

Should Travis tell Brynne where he was headed next? Should he tell her that he came clean with the sheriff? Should he offer to take her with him?

Too many questions, not enough good answers as far as he was concerned. At least he knew exactly where he stood with her mother. Ms. Beauden couldn't stand the ground he walked on, even when she owned it.

Since he might run into her anyway, he might as well tell her about his next move. "I'm heading to Lawler's office." And since she was going to ask why, he continued, "I told him about us."

"You did?" She didn't bother to hide the shock in her voice.

"It was going to come out anyway and since someone decided to drag my name into this whole mess, I decided to take the bull by the horns," he admitted.

"That was probably a smart idea," she reasoned.

"If this thing circled back to me again and the sheriff needed to investigate me, I didn't want him wondering why I didn't say anything before," he explained.

"No, I get it," she said. "I'm just...surprised, I guess."

"With everything going on in my family with the law, it was only a matter of time before someone asked if I was responsible, Brynne." He threw his hands up. "I was your first stop. Remember?"

"Because I knew about the bandana and you had reason to be mad at me," she stated. "Those are the only reasons I came to you. I promise. I never would believe you intended to hurt me or my mother in any way. My temper got the best of me when I saw the bandana, but I wasn't mad at you."

"Sure as hell seemed that way."

"It's just everything," she said. "Life. It's been hell on wheels lately, like a runaway train and I have no power to slow it down or stop it." She flashed eyes at him. "But you have, too. So, there's no excuse for me unloading on you this morning. I should have known better and I'm sorry for barging onto your property with the accusation."

Didn't that take most of the fight out of him?

"Your apology is accepted," he said. "I'd like to help figure out who was behind the prank, if that's what we're dealing with. If it's more than that, I'd like to help put a stop to it."

"To clear your name?" she asked.

"Because I actually care what happens to you and your mother," he said a little more heated than he'd intended. "I wouldn't be able to sleep at night if I looked away now and something happened to either one of you."

Brynne blinked. "You'd look out for us even though my mother has been very clear about her feelings toward you?"

"Why wouldn't I?" he asked. "The weekend we spent together might not have meant anything to you, but I don't sleep with someone and then turn my back on them."

She didn't ask, *Even if they deserve it*, but it was written all over her expression. The fact she felt bad about treating him the way she did confirmed he hadn't wasted his time with someone who had no soul. It also didn't mean the two of them had to hate each other.

Was his ego bruised? Hell yes. But that wouldn't stop him from looking out for a neighbor.

"It's what ranchers do," he added in case she got any wild ideas he was in love with her and would stalk her at the first sign of a green light. "We take care of each other."

"Cowboy code," she said quietly.

"Something like that," he agreed. It ran deeper and had been ingrained in him since birth. "Plus, your mother has been to hell and back lately. I wouldn't hold much against her at this point."

Damn. Was that being hypocritical when he couldn't find it in his heart to forgive his own mother? He didn't exactly have history with Brynne's mother like his own. Although to be fair, she wasn't much of a mother. She'd checked out of that job a long time ago. It was still beyond him why she'd had nine children when she didn't intend to care for them.

And his father was just as much to blame. He'd married a trophy wife and then...what? Tried to outdo his brother by having the same number of children?

"It's true that my mother isn't herself right now, Travis. But that doesn't give her the right to be mean to you when you've been nothing but kind."

"I wouldn't sweat it if I were you," he countered. "I'm not."

"Why do you have to stop by the sheriff's?" she asked.

"To sign a waiver to give him permission to access my phone records," he said.

"I'm sorry," she said again. "I should have responded to you, but I was so messed up."

He didn't need her pity party. "Like I said, it's fine. Is it embarrassing? Yes. Does it bruise my ego to have another human read texts and listen to phone messages meant for your eyes only? Hell yes. But last I checked, no one died from embarrassment."

"No. No one did," she agreed. "And I doubt anyone ever will. But that doesn't mean I'm any less sorry for treating you the way I did."

"I appreciate the apology," he said. "Like I already said, I accept. There's nothing to go back and fix at this point. You were going through a rough patch. We spent a weekend together. It was just as good for me as I think it was for you. Besides, I think we both needed an escape from reality for a little while."

"Yes, but—"

"Let's move on, Brynne," he said emphatically. The last thing he wanted to do was keep rehashing the past or hear her apologize one more time for a weekend that he wouldn't forget for the rest of his life. The rest of his life? That might be dramatic. Still. It had been a damn good escape. The feel of her silky skin was burned into his memory, into his fingertips as he'd lazily ran them along the curves of her hips. And he also touched her not so lazily. Just touched her.

Her lips had tasted a lot like honeysuckle in late spring. Her body had moved with his in a rhythm so perfect that just thinking about it distracted the hell out of him. Don't even get him started on how he felt buried inside of her, when nothing mattered but the two of them and her warm, giving body.

Travis cleared his throat. "I need to head out. Do you want to ride with me? Follow me?"

He also noted how quickly she was able to stuff her feelings down deep before giving him a ride home. She'd become a little too good at distancing herself from her emotions. To the point of shocking him.

The thing he'd noticed about emotions, was stuffing them down never did any good. They had to come out eventually. And, in his experience, it was like a volcano erupting. There was no predicting when the thing would blow.

Which also reminded him to keep his distance. He understood why Brynne's emotions would be on edge considering everything she was going through with her mother, but that didn't mean he intended to be on the receiving end.

"Could we eat something first?" Brynne asked, catching him off guard again.

"Do you want to come inside my house or go somewhere?" he asked. He could whip up something. A sandwich was easy enough.

"I need to use the ladies' room," she said. "Mind if I come in?"

The last thing Travis expected at this point was for Brynne Beauden to waltz inside his home. Since he was being thrown curveball after curveball today, he said, "Why the hell not."

~

Brynne parked on the parking pad next to Travis's truck. Her bladder seemed to have turned into the size of a pea. She hoped the morning sickness was done with her for the day as she followed Travis inside his house.

"Which way?" she asked, figuring she could get the two-cent tour once she'd emptied her bladder.

He pointed to a water closet off the living room and then kept walking toward the open concept kitchen.

It didn't take long to take care of business. Brynne washed her hands and started to turn away. The image in the mirror stopped her cold. She was a mess. Her hair looked like it hadn't seen a brush today and the bags underneath her eyes had turned into dark circles. No blush or lipstick left her skin looking pale and washed out.

This shouldn't bother her as much as it did.

Brynne didn't wear a lot of makeup, but she probably had tinted lip gloss in her handbag somewhere. She didn't get a whole lot of dateable men randomly showing up at the farm, and she'd left this morning in a fit of anger. *Get a grip, Brynne.*

Digging around in her purse, her fingers closed around a tube that she hoped was fresh lip gloss. She pulled her hand out. *Bingo*. She shook the small bottle and then dipped the tip in and out a couple of times before applying the pink tint to her top lip and then the bottom. She compressed her lips, rubbed them together, and decided this was better than before.

What else could she do?

Pinching her cheeks brought some blood back to them. *Better.*

At the bottom of her handbag, she found an old rat-tailed comb and a packet of extra-strength mints. *Double score*. She ran the comb underneath the faucet as she turned the water on. After running the comb through her hair and deciding this was about as good as it was going to get, for better or worse, she tossed the items back inside her purse, popped a mint in her mouth, and exited the bathroom.

She wasn't sure how much better she looked, but she felt

a whole lot better. A lot more human. Funny how the little things meant so much in stressful circumstances.

Travis's home was exactly what she would expect of him. The living room was centered around a stone fireplace that had a flatscreen TV mounted above the mantel. A sound bar sat on the wood beam for a mantel and not much else. It was simple but it worked. The seating area consisted of two deep brown suede couches facing each other with a hand-carved wooden coffee table. It looked made from the same wood as the mantel.

There was a bench opposite the fireplace that looked suitable for sitting. The couches were oversized and looked comfortable. In fact, Brynne would like nothing more than to put her feet up on one of the right now. She could envision sinking into one of those babies with all those comfortable-looking pillows.

The end tables had brass sculptures from an artist she recognized. They were expensive, but you wouldn't know it to look at them; there were lamps that gave the place a homey feel. The living room gave way to the dining area on one side and the kitchen straight back.

Travis's head was presently stuck inside the fridge as he pulled out ingredients. "Club sandwich sound good?"

She remembered the ones he'd made and served while she was still in bed in Austin.

"Great," she said, hearing the frog in her own throat. She cleared her throat and tried again. "Yes. Good."

Brynne had to acknowledge the fact she couldn't go back and change the past. Travis might never want to see her face again once they figured out what was going on with the crop circle—and assuming the pregnancy didn't make it full term —but she could try.

"Did your mother say what your ex wanted when he

came by the house?" Travis asked, busy making sandwiches. At this point, she wished she had something to do with her hands. Right now, she twisted her fingers together in a knot, much like her stomach.

"We didn't get that far," Brynne admitted. She'd been too busy stressing that her mother figured out she was pregnant, but there was no way she was sharing that information with Travis. "She gets confused, so there's a chance he never even showed up. Her timelines get messed up." Was that wishful thinking? Probably. "I'm thinking he would have stayed until I got home, if he came all this way to see me. Right?"

"Makes sense to me," he said, his back turned to her. Some folks might say that was a sign of trust. Why did she automatically assume he didn't want to look at her? "You could find out one way or the other if you called him."

The thought of hearing Ty's voice right now sent a cold chill racing down her spine. "Or, it could remind him of a breakup that he didn't want."

"That's true too," Travis said.

"I'd hate to dredge up the past while the dirt is still fresh on the grave," she stated. Was she being morbid? Dramatic? The answer to both of those questions was probably yes. She needed to chill.

"I guess," he said.

"You know what I mean," she explained. "I'm the one who broke it off even though the relationship played out a long time ago. We both knew it. It's obvious when you don't see each other for weeks on end or talk so much as a couple times a week." Was she overexplaining?

But Travis needed to know she was long over Ty before the weekend in Austin and that he wasn't a rebound.

She almost laughed out loud at the thought of someone

as gorgeous and intense as Travis Firebrand being anyone's rebound.

There'd been no resuscitating her and Ty's relationship. The only reason she let it go on as long as she did was because Ty was always too tired to really talk. There was always some excuse for not being around each other more. At first, she'd believed there was someone else. That he was seeing someone and didn't have the heart to tell her. But, no, there wasn't. And she'd had to be the bad guy by saying the words, *it's over*.

"I get it," he said before turning around with two plates in hand. He motioned toward the granite island, where four bar chairs were pushed up on one side.

Brynne claimed a seat and Travis sat next to her. Trills of awareness skittered across her skin with him this close. She would blame her body's reaction to him on hormones, but it would be a flat-out lie. Travis had this effect on her. Still had the effect on her.

How much was he going to hate her if the pregnancy stuck?

The sandwiches were gone in a matter of minutes. Both of them were hungrier than they'd realized. Brynne chased the food with a large glass of milk, which caught Travis's eye. He, on the other hand, made a to-go cup of coffee. They were back on the road in minutes. Being with Travis was easy. Talking to Travis was surprisingly easy. She reminded herself not to get too used to this 'easy', because she might have to drop a bomb on the man. This was a no-win situation. Guilt was already consuming her.

"What's wrong?" he asked as he navigated into the parking lot of the sheriff's office.

"What? Nothing," she said quickly. Too quickly?

"You always get that wrinkle in your forehead when

you're stressed about something," he said. "I get that the current circumstances are stressful, and I understand what you're going through with your mother, but I get the feeling this is something different."

"It's what you said, stress," she confided in a partial truth. She was distressed about those things and another very big thing. Now was not the time to discuss it, though. Spend much more time around Travis and she might have to worry whether or not her mother figured her out. He might.

The thought terrified her.

His gaze dipped from her face to her stomach, where she realized her hands rested.

Brynne bit back a curse. Did she just give herself away?

9

"Ready?" Brynne asked, looking a little too eager to leave the truck and exit their current conversation.

"Sure," Travis said, dragging out the word before exiting the driver's side and then circling around the front of the truck to open the door for her. He held out a hand, which she took. And then he paused. He had questions. Was this the right time?

She reached up to touch the back of her neck as she surveyed the lot. Was she looking for something suspicious? Right here at the sheriff's office?

"All good?" Travis asked, studying her once again.

"I just got a creepy feeling," she admitted, trying to shake it off. "It's probably nothing." Was it wishful thinking on her part? Based on her expression, he assumed it might be. "We should go inside."

"Okay," Travis said, scanning the sprinkling of vehicles, looking for what had her riled up. "This shouldn't take long."

"And then what?" she asked. "There's no way I'll get any work done today and I don't want to be alone right now."

"I can stick around until you feel safe again." Travis reached for her hand, and then linked their fingers. Electricity hummed through his hand and then his arm at contact. You'd think he would be used to it by now, but she was special.

"Thank you," she said, momentarily leaning into him. He liked having her this close more than he wanted to admit. "Maybe the sheriff will have aerial photos of the crop circle to show us," he offered as they approached the door. "And then maybe we could head back to my house."

"Sounds like I plan. I'm drawing a blank on talking to anyone else about this, so we might as well call it for the day after this pitstop."

"The sheriff might be able to give us a clue as to who might be responsible at this point," Travis said, but this was wishful thinking on his part this soon in an investigation. Unless, of course, someone stepped forward, which was about as likely as a banker to offer twenty percent interest on a savings account.

"I've never been scared to be on the farm with Mother, just the two of us, before now," Brynne admitted as they walked toward the lobby of the sheriff's office. Her words punched him in the gut.

"I can stay overnight if it'll make you rest easier," he said, knowing full well her mother wouldn't put up with a Firebrand in the house. "Since your mother isn't exactly my biggest fan, I can sleep in my truck to make sure no one messes with the crops tonight or decides to escalate."

"No, you won't," she quickly countered. "I won't have that if you're helping us out. Mom will just have to get over herself."

"Does that mean you want me to stay?"

She nodded. "If you don't mind."

"It's no trouble," he said. "There's no one expecting me at home anyway. I can let everyone know I'll be late for work in the morning. We don't exactly punch a timecard at the ranch, but we're all needed to pitch in every day to keep the cattle safe and healthy, as well as keeping poachers off the land."

"I forget that's a problem for you guys," she said as he opened the door to the lobby. "Our worst nightmare is much smaller."

He drew his eyebrows together for a split second before the answer came to him. "Insects."

"That's right," she said. "Sometimes, the enemy is almost too small to see with the naked eye."

"I get that," he said. "We had a mysterious illness run through the calves during the season recently. Everyone was on edge until we got it under control and brought the herd back to health."

"Lives like ours are unpredictable," she said.

"And subject to Mother Nature's kindness," he added. "When she unloads a temper tantrum, the effects can wipe out people like us."

"I've always liked that about farming," she admitted. "The unpredictable nature of it. Knowing that we're really just a small speck in a big universe, and not everything is within our control. It reminds me that there's something so much bigger out there. Does that make sense or do I sound like I've lost it?"

"Yes, it does," he agreed. "It's one of the reasons I love being outside, camping. Granted, you know exactly what the weather is going to be like in August. Hot as hell. But in winter and spring, you never know what you're going to get.

The weatherperson doesn't know much better than any one of us. They might offer an educated guess, but Texas weather has a mind of its own. Apparently, it doesn't listen to these forecasts." He smiled, appreciating the break in tension.

The sheriff's office was a two-story building of nondescript, brown bricks with tall, thin windows.

"Is the sheriff in?" Travis asked as they stepped into the lobby and toward a reception desk to the left-hand side.

"He is, Mr. Firebrand and Ms. Beauden. He's expecting you," the older lady with all gray hair stated with pride. Travis couldn't remember her name and was too embarrassed to ask. Dotty? She stood up and waved for them to follow.

Then, she used her ID to badge them into a secure area where the hallway forked. One side held the offices and the other was the way to the jail based on the signs. Travis didn't want to think about being led down toward the jail. He shouldn't be so relieved the older woman turned toward the offices.

"I have the waiver you need to sign," she said. "It's at my desk, but the sheriff thought you might want to see the aerials right away."

"He read my mind," Travis agreed. Was this a sign the sheriff found something interesting? Something that might lead them to the answers they were searching for?

The older woman led them to a doorway before announcing them and then disappearing the same way she came.

"Sheriff," Travis said as Brynne's phone went off inside her purse. As she scrambled to answer, the sheriff's secretary came through on the intercom.

"Sir, you have an important call," she said. "I apologize

for the interruption but the person insists you'll want to take this."

Brynne managed to find her cell and then checked the screen. "It's my mom. I should probably answer."

The sheriff nodded as Brynne stood up and stepped away from the sitting area across from the sheriff's desk. He looked to Travis. "Do you mind if I take this?"

"Not at all," Travis replied. "Should I step out?"

"I won't know unless I answer," Sheriff Lawler said.

"Alright," Travis stated. "By all means." He gestured toward the desk phone.

"Who's calling?" the sheriff asked his secretary.

"Hector Jugo," she said. "He's working at Ms. Beauden's place today."

Travis was to his feet in a heartbeat. The phone call from Brynne's mother must be the same reason as Hector's call to the sheriff. The fact her mother was calling was a good thing. Because his mind immediately snapped to something happening to her while Brynne was gone.

"What's going on, Mom?" Brynne asked, concern steeped in her voice. She turned to face Travis and locked gazes as he stepped into the hall with her. "Okay." She paused a couple of beats. "I'm at the sheriff's office." Another few beats of silence. "I can be home in less than half an hour if I leave now." The color drained from her face. "Don't go anywhere near it. Okay?"

Brynne ended the call, promising to get home. Travis figured the sheriff was about to follow them, so he popped his head inside the office.

"We're heading out now," he said to the sheriff. "Meet you there?"

"Yep," the sheriff said to him before moving his mouth back to the receiver.

Travis reached for Brynne's hand and then linked their fingers as he made a beeline for his truck. He didn't bother to stop at the lobby desk to sign the consent and he didn't ask what was going on. He knew they needed to get back as fast as possible and they would have close to thirty minutes in the truck. Brynne could give him the rundown then. Based on her expression, something serious was going down.

BRYNNE COULD KICK herself for leaving her mother alone. She darted toward Travis's truck, hand-in-hand. Physical contact kept her from going into full-on panic mode. And she was one hundred percent certain her body wouldn't react the same to anyone else. Travis was calm under pressure. He kept a cool head and faced danger head on. She wasn't a wilting flower by any stretch of the imagination. She'd taken self-defense classes so she would never feel helpless. And that's just exactly what she felt right now. The feeling angered her to no end.

Once on the road, speeding toward her farm, she gave Travis the rundown. "A butchered calf was found on my farm."

"Who found it?"

"Hector," she supplied. "He's trustworthy. He's one of the people I rely on to vouch for other day laborers."

"Where is your mother?"

"Inside the house," she explained. "Hector took her to the site where he found the calf." She shook her head. "Anyone who hurts a helpless animal deserves to be strung by their..."

It was probably best not to finish the sentence. Hurting something so innocent was even worse.

"Agreed," was all he said in response. The low growl to his voice said five minutes alone with the sonofabitch was all Travis would need to demonstrate what it was like to feel pain.

She reached over and touched his arm as he white-knuckled the steering wheel. "Travis, the calf has been branded Firebrand."

He released a string of swearwords that would make a grandmother disown him if they were related, but they were the same ones Brynne was thinking. And the reason grandmothers popped into her head right then was because of something else her mother said on the phone.

"My grandparents are on their way over to the farm," she continued.

"I'm guessing they like me about as much as your mother does."

"You'd be right." She didn't deny it. "Not that their opinion matters much to me. My mom said she panicked and told them everything when they called to see if the crop circle was true. They have a way of finding information, getting under her skin, and making her feel like she has to confess. They'll try to take the farm and convince her to move in with them so they can take care of her if she opens up about her diagnosis, which was another reason we've been tight-lipped about it."

"Your mother wouldn't do that," he said. "Would she?"

"Not if I'm there to stop it." Wasn't it bad enough they'd offered no support all these years? Did they actually have to make matters worse? Showing up like they were the cavalry when they'd done nothing but abandon Brynne and her mom when they needed support the most. "I have news for them. I'm a grown woman capable of taking care of my mom during the later phases of the disease and the farm. I've been doing most of the work longer than I care to remember anyway."

"This is probably not the time to ask, but did you even want to own a farm? When you were younger? Because it seems like I remember you had other plans. And you already said you wanted to be an artist, so what happened?"

"No, to answer your first question," she supplied, trying to hide her disappointment. "I haven't thought about making art my real career in too long. I'm too established in farm work to start another business anyway. And even if I wasn't, how would I do it? I haven't taken an art class in years. Haven't even seriously thought about another life since not long after I graduated high school." She could hear the defensiveness in her own voice.

"I wasn't trying to upset you with the question, believe it or not." He gripped the steering wheel tighter. "I just remember you used to carry around those handblown glass vases and they were the most beautiful things I'd ever seen."

"Are you serious?" She'd forgotten all about the dream of owning her own shop one day with a small gallery to sell her pieces out front. How could he have known? Remembered something she didn't about herself? "You really thought they were good?"

"Even the Marshal commented about them," he said. "Said he would pay good money for those, which was saying a lot coming from that old man. Then again, he collected bronzes and paintings, so it shouldn't surprise me that he would dabble in other art forms."

"Wow," she said, still feeling whiplash switching to this topic. "I guess I just don't have time for any of that anymore. I have a farm to run and a mother to take care of." She stopped herself right there, before mentioning anything about the baby.

"I'm surprised you don't think about it at all," he admitted. "You're too good at it to walk away."

"Would you jump ship and hit the rodeo circuit tomorrow if you could?" she asked, turning the tables. If he was going to call her out for not following her dream, turnabout was fair play.

"Nah," he said. "Rodeo is a pipe dream even though I sometimes try to convince myself it isn't. I made my peace with my choice, even though I do have regrets from time to time. But it was my choice to make. What about you, Brynne? Are you living someone else's dream or your own?"

Those words stung worse than a dozen bee stingers.

"Did you just judge me?" she asked, not bothering to mask her anger—anger that seemed always at the ready lately.

"Nah," he said casually. "Not a judgment. Just a couple of questions. I don't mean anything by it, Brynne. I know how important your mother is to you and making certain she has a partner in the farm is the honorable thing to do. I was just curious if you were living your dream or hers. I didn't mean any harm by it."

Then, why did the questions hit her in the center of the chest? *Because they were true?*

"I can't think about art right now when my grandparents are on their way to the farm to convince a daughter they turned their backs on to move in with them," she quipped, forcing the conversation back on track. "Whatever they intend to try isn't going to work. I'll make certain of it."

"What if they have the free time to take care of your mom and want to right a wrong from the past?"

"Are you saying that I'm not doing a good enough job?"

she asked. "Because I'm exhausted from taking care of everyone else. But I'll keep doing it because that's what my mom needs. That's what family does for each other."

"I'm playing devil's advocate here, but what if they're sorry for their past actions, Brynne? What then? Would you let them back in your life? Step aside so your mother could let them back in hers?" His questions felt like bullets, even though his voice was calm and reassuring.

He was also being a hypocrite.

"How about you, Travis?" she asked. "Have you forgiven your mother?"

"We're not talking apples to apples here, Brynne. My mother attempted to kill someone for financial gain. She also turned her back on her family, by the way."

"True. What makes you the angriest? The fact your mother tried to hurt another human being or the fact she turned her back on her family all those years ago?" she continued, despite how uncomfortable the shift in conversation made him. If he could dish it out, he could take it as far as she was concerned.

"Both," he admitted after a thoughtful pause. "Your turn."

Well, didn't that just throw a wrench in her plans?

10

Before the conversation could go further, Travis was pulling into the long driveway of the farm. He'd answered questions that stirred up feelings in him that he wasn't ready to deal with. Feelings about his mother. His father. The Marshal. Why were family relationships so complicated?

On the outside, they could look perfect. Perfect kids. Perfect marriage. Perfect life. But the minute the layers were peeled back, the fantasy busted wide open. This was one of many reasons he never intended to go down the aisle. His brothers and cousins who were married or in the process might look happy now. But wouldn't they all end up like his brother Kellan? Divorced, broken, and alone?

Look what marriage had done to him. It had shredded his heart. Some family members joked it had been proof he had a heart. Kellan could be cold-blooded. But then what had he expected when he fell in love with the love of his cousin's life? Didn't that immediately spell heartbreak and disappointment down the line? The worst part was that Kellan had swooped in during a crisis moment for Liv, now

Corbin's wife. Her mother had just died and she must have felt sad and alone. One glance at Brynne and her mother's relationship told him all he needed to know about the bond between a mother and daughter when it was good. Liv had been very close with hers.

The sun was setting by this point, and darkness was settling in. He grabbed a flashlight from the back of his truck after opening the door and helping Brynne step down.

Ms. Beauden paced on the porch. The minute she saw her daughter, she started toward her. Even from this distance, he could see the worried look on her face as she approached.

A silver Cadilac was parked next to the home. An elderly couple sat in the rocking chairs, leaning forward. The woman he assumed to be Brynne's grandmother was fiddling with something in her hands. He couldn't tell what it was from this distance. Knitting? Crocheting? Whatever it was, it was pink.

Ms. Beauden wrapped her arms around her daughter as though she was a life raft and the older Beauden was drowning.

"Where is Hector?" Brynne asked once her mother had felt enough reassurance to take a step back.

"He's out in the field where the..." She glanced from Brynne to Travis. "I know you would never hurt one of your own animals. I'm sorry this has happened to your livestock."

"Thank you," he said, figuring that apology covered a lot of ground. His cell started buzzing. He glanced at the screen. Speaking of Kellan, his older brother was firing off texts. Travis tucked the phone in his pocket for the time being and then looked up at Ms. Beauden. "I'll find the bastard responsible and make certain justice is served." He stopped himself there before he said other words he might regret in mixed company. He'd been brought up better than to swear in front of his elders, but this situation called for it.

"He's staying over tonight, Mom," Brynne interjected. "I don't want to be on the farm by ourselves."

"Is that a good idea, Brynne?" her mother asked, glancing down at her stomach and then making a face.

What did she know?

"We have to go see the scene," Brynne said to her mother before grabbing Travis's hand and practically dragging him away. "Point us in a direction."

"Near the creek by the place you used to camp," her mother said.

"Okay," Brynne stated, pulling on his hand as she led the way.

Travis had questions about what Ms. Beauden was referring to, but they had to be shelved for now. One of his calves had been senselessly killed, which worried him on more than one level. Was there a serial killer in the making in the once-sleepy town of Lone Star Pass? Someone threatening Brynne and her mother? Again, he circled back to the question of who would want to scare the Beaudens?

Behind the farmhouse was a small yard and a trail that led to a creek. Hector was kneeling down, examining the calf. The pungent smell hit Travis first. Brynne grabbed her stomach. Was she about to lose her lunch?

"Why don't you let me take a look?" Travis said to her, stopping. She couldn't move him if she tried but she didn't. Instead, she leaned into him. Physical contact reminded his body of just how much pleasure there'd been when the two of them touched. Not a good idea. Not that it mattered much out here. The smell alone would douse any fire lit inside him.

"Okay," she finally said. She was used to running

things around the farm, so it was probably difficult for her to step aside and let someone else handle a situation on her property. He took it as a compliment she yielded to him.

"Do you want to wait over there?" He pointed toward an area of thicker trees that would place her downwind from the stench.

"Okay," she said again. Her skin was already losing color. He had no idea she had such a queasy stomach. But then, what did he really know about her after a weekend together?

A voice in the back of his mind wanted to argue that he'd gotten to know her in the biblical sense. What did it matter if he didn't know her favorite color or what she liked on a pizza? Because weren't those the little things that made up a relationship?

Again, the voice wanted to argue. He shut it down before he changed his mind and asked her out again. How ridiculous did that make him?

∼

"I HAVE TO ASK," Brynne said to Hector, as he walked toward her. "The sheriff thinks one of the guys might be responsible for the crops and I'm guessing he'll have the same thought about this crime. What do you think? Did my mom do something to upset one of the men?"

Hector stood five-feet-six-inches. He always wore a white Stetson, no matter the season, because he decided good cowboys always wore white hats. She didn't have the heart to tell him the color of the Stetson depended on the season and not the cowboy's heart. He was honest, hardworking, and had been coming back to the farm as a seasonal worker almost ten years straight. He was the closest thing they had to a loyal employee.

"I don't think so, miss," he said. No matter how many times she asked the older man to call her by her first name, he refused. Said it was a bad example for the other men. So, she was miss to him instead of Brynne. "I know Mateo and Santiago like they were my brothers. Neither of them would do anything like this. As for Chris and James, they're friends of Santiago. He wouldn't recommend anyone he didn't trust, but you never can be one hundred percent about people. You know? I can talk to them."

"The sheriff is going to want to speak to them too," she said, but Hector was already shaking his head.

"Santiago will disappear before he'll speak to the sheriff," Hector said.

"I thought everyone was legal to work," she stated.

"They are." He lifted his hat high enough to scratch his head. "But Santiago is behind on child support. He's paranoid that he'll end up in jail and then he'll be in a bigger hole. His car broke down, and his mother's check is late. That's why he got behind."

"Does he really think the law will snap him up that fast and arrest him? It doesn't sound like he's very behind on support," she pointed out. "Wouldn't they be able to give him a break and give him more time?"

"The state doesn't mess around. And he's been behind for months now," he said. "His ex is threatening him. He's doing his best and she has a job. She's bringing in enough to get by." Hector shook his head. "Once you get behind, the hole becomes deeper and it gets harder to catch up." He paused before making eye contact. "I wouldn't want to be in the position to choose whether not to keep a roof over my mother's head or send money to my child."

"That's awful," Brynne agreed, instinctively moving her hands to her belly before catching herself and lifting them high enough to cross them over her chest like she was suddenly cold. Why was it when you thought of something you shouldn't do, it automatically became your go-to?

"I have to warn him," Hector said.

That was going to be a problem. "The sheriff will be pulling up any minute, Hector. He'll think you have something to hide and that won't look good for either one of you."

The feeling of being watched caused the tiny hairs on the back of her neck to prick once again. She surveyed the area. It was too dark to see very far. Crickets chirped louder this time of night as an eerie feeling settled over her.

There was no one in sight. Didn't mean no one was out there. An icy chill raced up her spine at the thought the person who did this could be out there, watching. Waiting? Enjoying striking fear inside her.

Rather than give the bastard the satisfaction, she forced her shoulders back and stood up straighter.

"You haven't seen anyone hanging around the farm, have you?" she asked Hector.

He shrugged after rubbing his chin. "No, miss. No one." Something dawned on him. "The one you used to go with was here to see your mother. He didn't look too happy when he left. He spit up gravel from his tires."

The dust cloud that formed with such a move was the reason folks called fights *dustups*. Oftentimes, they led to someone hopping in their truck and kicking up a bunch of gravel on the way out.

This also confirmed Ty and her mom had had words. Was her mom confused on what was said? Or hiding something?

"I just found out he was here," she admitted as Travis stood up, studied the ground, and then walked over. He'd taken quite a few pictures, no doubt to study later.

"Thank you, Hector," she said, not wanting to continue talking about Ty in front of Travis. Besides, this wasn't new information. She could tell him about the dustup later when she informed the sheriff. "You should probably head up to the house and wait. We'll stay here."

"Will do, miss," Hector said after acknowledging Travis. The two shook hands and then Hector disappeared.

"How bad is it?" she asked Travis, referring to the poor calf. The thought of it being killed made her stomach churn.

"As awful as you'd imagine." Thankfully, he left it at that. "I'm beginning to think there's some kind of cult involved here."

"Maybe the crop pictures will tell us something," she reasoned. "I'm guessing they were significant enough for the sheriff to want to show them to us. They must mean something."

Travis shook his head. "I wish I had answers."

A twig snapped to their left. Under normal circumstances, Brynne wouldn't panic. She knew there were all kinds of wildlife out here that could be slipping past. Most of the time, the critter was more afraid of humans than the other way around.

This time?

Those tiny hairs stood at attention again.

Travis brought his index finger up to his lips, indicating they should be quiet. He didn't have to worry, the last thing she wanted to do was give away their exact location by talking. There was very little in the way of natural light and what was left was fading fast. He moved stealthily through the trees. In two seconds, he'd disappeared. How?

She remembered how dangerous poachers were and how good Firebrands were at tracking them. Those skills would come in handy now. Still, her heartbeat pounded the inside of her ribcage.

Alone in the thicket, she heard every noise. Her thoughts bounced around as she listened. The calf. The fact her ex and her mom had been in a big fight her mom hadn't seen fit to tell Brynne about.

What could they have possibly been fighting about? Did her mom ask him to come and then tell him about the...

Brynne covered her mouth so she wouldn't gasp. That had to be it. Her mom must have figured out the pregnancy and then told Ty because she believed he was the father. She could see her mom digging her heels in when he denied it was possible.

Would he seek revenge? Did he hate her that much after the breakup?

11

Travis crouched low to the ground, moving slowly across the unfamiliar turf. If he was on Firebrand land, this would be a lot easier. Based on the twig snap, he could be searching for a predator for all he knew. But he wasn't taking chances. A human killed the calf. That same human might be out here, lurking, ready to strike.

In a few moments, law enforcement would be on the scene. Was the person who did this enough of a risk-taker to stick around? He had to know the sheriff would be here. Was that part of the excitement for him?

The bastard.

A line had been crossed that there was no recovering from. As far as right and wrong went, this was clear. Other situations in his life were becoming muddier.

Reaching into his pocket, he pulled out a Swiss Army knife. The utility knife came in handy in all situations, especially when he left his pistol in the truck. This probably wasn't the time to regret that decision but he hadn't thought he would need it since they were meeting the sheriff. Speaking of whom, this perp had a lot of nerve watching them, considering he had to know the sheriff would soon follow.

And then he heard a blood-curdling scream. He recognized the voice immediately. *Brynne.*

Travis could kick himself for leaving her alone. He bit out a string of curse words that would make his grandmother wash his mouth out with soap if she was still alive.

Circling back, guilt nearly consumed him. By the time he made it back to the calf site, she was gone.

Panic gripped him as his muscles corded with tension and frustration. Travis forced a calm he didn't feel as he turned on the flashlight and checked for tracks.

From the looks of it, Brynne had been dragged away. She was quiet now, which stressed him to no end. Calling out to her would only give away his location and any element of surprise he had as a trick up his sleeve. So, he didn't.

Instead, he followed the tracks to the exact spot where the underbrush was too thick to leave a trail. At this point, broken limbs were his best bet. He cupped the flashlight as he heard the squawk of a law enforcement radio.

"Ms. Beauden?" Sheriff Lawler called out. He wasn't far from Travis.

"Over here," he responded when she didn't. "Hurry."

A few seconds later, Sheriff Lawler came through the trees close enough for Travis to get a good look at him.

"Brynne's gone and we don't have much time to find her," he said, giving the two-second version of what had just happened. "I followed the trail here, where it ends."

Nightfall wasn't the ideal time to hunt someone without any equipment to level the playing field. At least he had the sheriff now. Maybe Hector wasn't too far. Could he circle back and help with the search? They needed all hands on deck.

"Can you call Ms. Beauden and ask to speak to Hector?" Travis asked, hating that with every second that ticked by, Brynne was being moved farther away from them. Did someone have a vehicle stashed? Would they toss her inside and disappear?

A flood of emotions tried to suck Travis under but he couldn't let them.

The sheriff made the call. Hector agreed to get in on the search and he rounded up one of the farm hands who'd stayed behind. With four of them, they'd just increased their odds of finding Brynne. He could only pray she would be unharmed when they did.

"I'll follow this trail," Travis said to the sheriff. "It might be a trick to lead us away but it's all I've got."

"Stay in touch," Sheriff Lawler pleaded. "I'm calling you right now. Turn the volume down and I'll do the same."

"Got it," Travis said before heading out. He tucked the cell in the front pocket of his shirt after turning down the screen's light. The last thing he needed was for the thing to give away his location at the wrong moment. Wasn't that how life worked? Timing was everything and his had been less than stellar.

But he couldn't dwell on that right now. Not with Brynne out there being dragged through the trees.

Dragged. That was it. He dropped down onto all fours and put his ear to the ground after clearing enough underbrush to put ear to dirt.

If he listened carefully, he could hear footsteps if they were anywhere near the vicinity of his location. The sheriff's would be to his left, away from the home. Hector would be coming from the right, but he wasn't close enough yet to pick up on his.

Travis got nothing. Which either meant the bastard

stopped walking or carrying or dragging Brynne. Hiding? Or they were too far away to pick up on the sound of their footprints.

It was getting late and cold was settling in. So was anger. Followed by determination.

Travis bit back a curse and popped to his feet. All he could do was march ahead, silently and stealth-like. He was good at this. He'd honed his tracking skills on his family's ranch. He told himself this would be no different.

Could he get to Brynne in time? Or was he already too late? Because another answer—one he didn't want to consider—was that she was lying out here somewhere, already dead.

How long was this bastard hiding and watching? Waiting for the right moment to strike?

∼

ALL FIVE OF Brynne's senses had been taken away from her as she was dragged through the trees. Some type of cloth bag came over her head after her mouth was taped shut. Hearing was muffled because of the bag, as was her sense of smell. But first, she'd been hit over the head and knocked out cold. Right now, everything was still. Quiet.

She wanted to scream but the bastard who did this to her believed she was still unconscious. It was best to keep it that way. The sounds of heavy breathing sent rockets of fear spiraling through her. Maybe the guy would mutter something under his breath to give her a hint as to his identity. Or, while she was wishing, maybe he would speak and she would recognize his voice.

At this point, he could be anyone.

Random thoughts came to mind. Her birth father? Why

would he want to scare Brynne and her mom? Better yet, why would he come back and abduct Brynne? Didn't he realize he could call her up and see her without the fear of being arrested and jailed for nonsupport a very long time?

Strange how he was almost always the first person who came to mind when she thought about a man. She didn't even know him or where he lived. For all she knew he could be dead or living in South Dakota. Why South Dakota? Again, she had no good answer as to why that came to mind. All she knew about the man was that his parents were from South Dakota. They were long since dead but he'd spent half of his childhood there before they'd moved to Texas. She always assumed he went back to South Dakota after ditching her mom. After ditching her.

Good or bad, he was the first person who popped into her thoughts.

After hearing about the dustup between her mom and Ty, she had questions about him too. But he wouldn't hurt her. Would he?

Her brain hurt.

Beyond those two men, she had no idea who could possibly be involved. The sheriff might be right about the workers. Santiago? Would he do something like this? Was he desperate for money? Would he abduct her for ransom?

She might not have had deep conversations with him, but he'd always been honest and hardworking. Hector trusted him. Santiago was taking care of his mother and trying his best to do what was right by his child, from what Hector said. But then he was also in a difficult situation. Folks who felt trapped with their backs against the wall did terrible things.

Would he butcher a calf? Spread its blood around?

Fear tried to overtake her but she refused to give in. If

anything, she was more concerned about the pregnancy. Extreme situations had a tendency to bring out buried emotions, she'd noticed. A growing part of her hoped the pregnancy turned out to be viable. Not to mess with Travis in any way or force him into a situation he wanted nothing to do with—she would give him the option to be involved and he could do with it what he wanted—but because she wanted the little bean.

It had taken two to make this little bean and he had to know this was at least a possibility, even if no one ever believed it would happen to them. As far as being mentally prepared to have a kid, was anyone ever ready?

How the hell was she going to get away from this creep? Should she call out a name? See if she got a response? Something told her that if she called out the wrong one, the situation would end up far worse. Not that she could with her mouth covered.

A grunt was followed by her being dropped onto her side. She landed hard, a sharp object jammed into her hip.

She couldn't suppress her scream but the mouth covering did the job for her.

Next, there were footsteps. Running fast. She strained to hear as the sound grew weaker. Running away?

She tensed, unsure of what would happen next. None of this made sense. Was the bastard about to make sure she left these woods in a body bag?

Where did he go?

A sudden beam of light passed over her.

"Brynne?" Travis asked. His voice washed over her, giving her hope she might not die out here alone.

She did her best to speak, to scream but couldn't manage more than a mumble with whatever covered her mouth. Tape?

The next thing she knew, the sack was being pulled off her head. Then came the tape. It was ripped off in one quick motion that stung like hell. Her arms were next. They were bound behind her back. Her ankles were tied together with rope. The side of her hip hurt as did her back. Had she been pulled through part of the thicket?

The second her arms were free, she wrapped them around Travis's neck. He pulled her up to standing and looped his arms around her waist, ever watchful of their surroundings.

"Where are you hurt?" he asked, returning his gaze to hers before skimming her body with his eyes.

"I have a few scratches and bruises and my hip hurts like hell, but I'll be fine," she said before pressing a kiss to his lips—lips she'd dreamed about kissing again more than she cared to admit. "Thank you for finding me."

"Not finding you wasn't an option," he said before dipping his head down and tasting her lips one more time. "Who did this to you?"

"I don't know," she admitted. "I took a blow to the back of the head and everything after that is blank. By the time I regained consciousness a few minutes ago, he dropped me and ran." She brought her hand up to her head, expecting to feel wet liquid but instead found a knot on the crown. "There's no blood." Her arms were scraped and she was certain her left hip had a mother of a bruise on it. But that was the worst of it, and she counted herself lucky because of it. This could have been a whole lot worse.

Travis searched her eyes. Did he believe her?

"I thought I'd lost you for good," he said with the kind of fear that reached the depths of his soul.

"You're not getting rid of me that easily, Firebrand," she teased, because if she didn't, if she really thought about the gravity of the situation, she would fold up her tent and cry. Crying wouldn't do any good. It didn't solve a problem despite sometimes needing the release. "I heard footsteps running in that direction."

Travis pulled out his cell phone after moving the two of them behind a tree to put some mass in between them and the abductor. He unmuted the call with the sheriff and put the phone on speaker. "Brynne is safe and with me," he immediately stated. "You know the direction I headed?"

"Yes," Sheriff Lawler said.

"I traveled a straight line until I came upon her," he said. "No sign of the perp and she has no information about him either. She was knocked out cold. Only woke a couple of minutes ago."

"We know he has to be strong enough to drag or carry her through the thicket," Sheriff Lawler said. "I'm heading your way while we talk."

"That was my guess too," Travis said, ever watchful.

Brynne's knees shook and her body ached, but she'd be damned if she'd let the jerk who did this to her make her afraid of her own shadow. Glancing down, she realized she had a protective hand over her belly. Thankfully, Travis was focused elsewhere, distracted. She'd made the move enough since they'd been forced together that her main fear was that he would figure it out before she could tell him.

Would he resent her for that too?

She moved her hand to her lower back and took in a deep breath to calm her rattled nerves. Being this stressed couldn't be good for the baby. More than anything, she wanted to go home and put her feet up. Since that wasn't possible, she squatted down so she could sit on the backs of her heels.

Travis stood guard in a protective stance as he talked the sheriff to their location.

"Which way did he go?" Sheriff Lawler asked.

"The sound of his footsteps went that way, I believe." Brynne pointed.

Then, he offered Brynne a hand up. "I'm taking you back to the house."

The thought of going home was almost too good to be true. Brynne took Travis's hand and stood up.

"If he's out here, I'll find him," Sheriff Lawler reassured as he turned toward the direction she'd pointed a moment ago. "I have a deputy coming around from this way. We'll meet up soon and keep the search going."

"Thank you, Sheriff." Brynne paused. She wanted to ask about the aerial pictures. Decided this wasn't the time.

The bastard might still be out there. Would he strike again? This time hurt Brynne's mom?

Her hands fisted until Travis reached for hers and then linked their fingers. A sudden calm came over her with contact. And she desperately needed it.

12

The quicker Travis got Brynne out of the thicket and inside her home, the better. He already didn't like the fact she'd been knocked out. He wanted to get a doctor to take a look at her as soon as possible. Plus, she'd been acting strange all day, looking like she might vomit several times. Was she coming down with something?

Based on her pale skin and queasy stomach, she was running herself ragged at the very least.

"I can carry you," he offered.

"No." She quickly shot him down. "I'm able to walk. I should walk."

"Suit yourself," he snapped, more irritation in his voice than he'd intended. He wasn't here to make her feel worse.

Travis bit his tongue so he wouldn't snap again. His stress shot through the roof and he wanted answers. He'd been so close to losing Brynne that he'd almost lost his mind.

They fast-walked toward the house through the thicket. Thankfully, she didn't let go of his hand despite his curt comment a minute ago. She faltered, almost tripping when the toe of her shoe got caught. He grabbed her elbow and held her upright in one swift motion.

Brynne was proud. In most cases, she wouldn't need or accept help. The fact she was more than willing to accept it now caused more concern than he wanted to admit. This was a far cry from the fiery woman who'd shown up at his house this morning. Damn. It felt like an eternity had passed. Had it really been less than twenty-four hours ago that she'd come roaring up in her Chevy?

From the clearing in the backyard, he could tell all the lights were on downstairs. The back porch light was on too. Her mother had to be worried sick.

Travis couldn't get her inside the house fast enough. In the light, he saw that her jeans were ripped on her left hip. He had to bite back his anger at the fact she'd been dragged through the underbrush, almost to her death.

"I thought you were..." Her mother stopped herself from finishing the sentence spoken the minute they stepped into the kitchen.

Brynne's grandparents sat at the kitchen table, gripping coffee mugs like they were buoys in a storm. Relief washed over the older couple the second Brynne walked into the room. Travis only hoped their presence wouldn't create more fireworks.

"I'm okay, Mom," Brynne said with a quick glance over at her grandparents.

"Thank heaven," her mother said as the two embraced.

"I'm safe now," Brynne said to her mother in the softest, most reassuring tone. "It's okay. We're okay. Travis found me in time. He scared the bastard off."

Ms. Beauden gasped. She brought a hand up to cover her mouth, while still hugging her daughter with the other arm.

When Brynne finally took a step back, her mother turned to Travis.

"Thank you for keeping my baby girl safe," Ms. Beauden said to him. He tried to shake off the shock so he could form a response.

"I'm just relieved I got there in time," he admitted.

Ms. Beauden made a beeline for him and threw her arms around him in a hug. "I wasn't very nice to you earlier and I'm sorry for my behavior. I'm too protective over my daughter sometimes. You'll understand soon enou... some day when you have children of your own."

"Yes, ma'am," he said as she took a step back and then sized him up.

"I don't know what I would have done if Brynne hadn't walked through the back door," she said. "From now on, you're family. Please, call me Jess."

"Yes, ma'am...*Jess*," he corrected.

"Thank you for saving our granddaughter," the older gentleman said. His words lit a fire in Brynne's eyes.

To her credit, she didn't speak. She didn't spew the hateful words that must be so readily available on her tongue.

"I need a shower and some water," Brynne said, fixing a glass. She made two and then handed one over to Travis. He downed his, wishing it was coffee instead. He had a long night ahead of him and could use the caffeine boost.

He must have made a face about the water because Ms. Beauden...Jess...offered to make him a cup of fresh brew.

"I'd appreciate that very much," he said to her.

He watched as she busied herself and realized she was probably grateful to have something to do with her hands— hands that shook as he provided an update. He couldn't imagine not being able to rely on his body to do what his brain told it to. Not being able to pick up a fork to feed himself. Or drive his vehicle. Jess Beauden wasn't to that point yet, but it was the future. It was coming as surely as extreme heat in summer months. He couldn't imagine the amount of dread a diagnosis like hers would cause. Then, the eventual fact she would lose all control over her muscles, her body functions.

He mentally shook off the horror.

It was unimaginable to him to be cursed with that fate. He relied on his hands and the rest of his limbs to be in tip-top shape for his livelihood in order to work the ranch. He could admit to taking his physical agility for granted. When he reached for a cup, his body obeyed with efficiency. The thought of slowly losing the ability to move around freely, like he did now, would set anyone into a depression.

All things considered, Jess Beauden was handling the diagnosis better than anyone could expect. She might be slipping down a depressive slope every once in a while, but she still had fight in her eyes.

Travis took the opportunity to introduce himself to Brynne's grandparents, who met him with a firm handshake and a hug. Both looked worried and beyond distressed. There were other emotions there too. Guilt? Shame?

Had they regretted walking away from their daughter and granddaughter all those years ago? Had too much time passed for them to find new ground for a relationship now? Jess had invited them over. Facing her own mortality would give her a reason to want a connection despite their history. If they were truly sorry for their actions, could the relationships be recovered? Could Brynne ever forgive them for calling her a bastard?

"I'm heading upstairs," Brynne stated, without so much as giving her grandparents the time of day. She didn't have a mean bone in her body. The snub was born out of years of hurt and self-protection. His own grandfather was a class-A jerk who'd run one of Travis's cousins out of town years ago when he found out about an unplanned teen pregnancy. Those rejections were next to impossible to move beyond, especially when they festered for years on end.

"My room is the first one on the left at the top of the stairs," Brynne continued, undaunted. "Once you get your coffee, will you meet me in there to go over my statement to Sheriff Lawler? I need to change out of these clothes."

Even with dirt in her hair and ripped clothes, she was beautiful. There was something different about her too. A glow?

Travis still half-expected her mother to kick him out. "Go ahead. I'll be right up."

Brynne nodded before disappearing.

Rather than read him the riot act or throw him out, Jess handed him a cup of coffee and then said she didn't want to keep him downstairs longer than she had to.

"Go on," Jess urged. "She needs a friend right now."

Jess's attitude toward Travis shifted fast enough to give him whiplash. Then again, her emotions were clearly all over the place. He'd never seen anyone downshift from outright hate to welcoming someone with open arms. It was clear to him, however, how much she loved her daughter. Their bond wasn't something every family had, and he envied them on some level for their closeness. The grandparent relationship, on the other hand, couldn't be more opposite.

Then again, growing up with a single mother must have made the two of them feel alone against the world.

The town could have been better about stepping up to the plate to support the two of them. He imagined there were a few who'd helped. Too many others were judgmental instead of compassionate.

Wasn't he becoming the town's conscience? Travis almost laughed as he excused himself. Or maybe he was becoming the town's protector?

Or was it just Brynne's protector?

Could he protect someone so strong-willed she infuriated him?

How could he not try?

~

A HOT SHOWER did good things to reset the brain. Clean clothes and a toothbrush were like Christmas morning to Brynne right now. She dressed in another pair of loose-fitting yoga pants and a sports bra, along with an oversized hoodie. Heaven. And hidden. There was no sign of her pregnancy yet. Lizzy reassured Brynne that was normal for a first time. Warm, fuzzy socks topped off her go-to comfort outfit.

Taking a deep breath, she headed into her bedroom, where Travis waited. She didn't need to see this man sitting on her bed like he belonged there. The visual was going to be impossible to erase as much as his imprint on her body and soul would be.

"Hey," she said to Travis, hearing the frog in her throat—a throat that tried up like the desert the minute she made eye contact with the gorgeous as sin rancher.

"Hey," he said back, his voice low and gravely. She chalked it up to circumstances. He was tired and the cold air probably got into his chest.

"Sorry about downstairs," she said. Sitting downstairs with her mom and grandparents wasn't something she could stand. How could her mother act like those people hadn't betrayed them, turned their backs on them, and then let them struggle for years? "I don't know why they're here."

Travis clamped his lips shut. Was he holding back what he really wanted to say?

They were going to have to be able to talk about just about everything if they shared a child. She needed to build some trust. Trust? She almost laughed out loud at the word. How would he ever trust her once he found out she'd been keeping this secret from him?

"It's okay," she said. "If you have an opinion about them. About me. About my non-relationship with them. You can speak your mind."

Travis put his hand in the air, palms up, in the surrender position. "I'm the last one who should judge or give advice to anyone else's family. Mine is so messed up, I don't even know where to start."

Brynne half smiled. "Guess we're not so different after all."

"Nope," he said. "I imagine every family has their secrets and dirty laundry. Mine is out there for everyone to see, so there's no hiding most of it."

"You're a Firebrand, Travis. That means something to this community."

"I'm a normal person too," he defended.

"I didn't mean it like that," she corrected. How should she say this? "No one ever cared about my mom and I; we could have starved to death for anyone knew. But your family was front and center of everyone's attention, as much for the jobs created and the generosity of your grandfather as to watch every move you guys made." It was her turn to put a defensive hand up. "I'm not saying your grandfather was a wonderful man by any stretch of the imagination. I didn't know him from Adam. Only what I overheard and saw. But he gave a lot of money to charity, and so the town revered him on many levels."

"He bought his place in society," Travis pointed out. "While treating his family like dirt. But he had everyone fooled, didn't he?"

"That might be true," she admitted. "The money still helped the Carvers when they got behind on their mortgage, because Guy got laid off and his wife was pregnant. They went to the Home for Hope charity that your family funded and were able to get back on their feet by the time the baby was born."

"Why is it so much easier to focus on the negative gossip?" he asked. The question had a wistful quality. "You know what I'm talking about. The big mouths who criticize and tear down. Why do they get to have space in our brains? Why is it so easy to believe everyone else is like they are? Watching your every move. Waiting for you to fail?"

"I don't know," she said, sitting down next to him. "You're right, though. I'm always worried about one snide comment, which I've heard quite a few over the years from people I thought were nice."

"If I've learned one thing living in Lone Star Pass my entire life, is that when folks tell you who they are, believe them," he stated.

"That's a good point," she said. "I guess that whole 'forgive others' bit keeps getting in the way. It's so ingrained in us that I don't even think about it."

"You can forgive someone, but still have their number," he pointed out. "Stops them from being able to keep hurting you. No one has a right to be given free access to us."

Brynne thought about it for a few seconds. "You're right, you know."

"Say those words again," he teased, "but a little louder this time."

She playfully tapped him on the arm, and basically met a brick wall of muscle. "Ouch." She withdrew her hand in dramatic fashion, scrunching her face like she'd just been punched.

Travis took her hand. "Let me see this."

His touch sent sensual shivers racing up her arm, flooding her chest with warmth.

"Where does it hurt?" he asked, that low, husky voice traveling over her.

She couldn't find her voice.

He ran a finger along her palm. "Here?"

She could barely manage a nod.

He pressed a kiss to the flat of her palm, then feathered others on her fingertips. An ache formed in her chest. The same one she'd experienced in Austin. The one that had scared the bejesus out of her and made her rethink everything she thought she knew about falling in love before spending time with Travis.

In love?

The idea she could be deeply in love with someone, after only spending one weekend together had shocked the hell out of her. The notion someone could literally shatter her heart into a thousand tiny flecks of dust after being together such a short time had made her jerk her hand away from any possible flame. The belief this man, Travis Firebrand, could hold her heart in his hands if he wanted to left her feeling too vulnerable.

She'd panicked. She'd ghosted him. She'd been a horrible person.

And now she might regret those actions for the rest of her life. Because what if he'd been *the one* and she'd been too worried about protecting her heart to open it up? What if the two of them had been fated to meet in Austin so she could see what real love was like after settling far too long? What if she'd walked away from the one person who could make her happy for the long haul?

"Travis," she started, finally finding her voice again. She wanted to explain everything. To tell him that she'd been too scared of having her heart broken to return his calls or texts. To tell him that she wanted to believe everything would magically work out but couldn't find the way. To tell him that she wished she'd given them a chance because her new fear was that she'd just thrown away the best thing that had ever happened to her.

What was stopping her?

Brynne opened her mouth to speak when her mom screamed. Before she could push to standing, she knew the reason.

The smell of smoke immediately brought out a coughing fit.

Fire.

13

Travis was on his feet in two seconds flat. The smell of smoke filled the room surprisingly fast, coming from somewhere downstairs.

"Fire, Brynne," Jess shouted upstairs before a coughing jag. "Get out of the house. Now."

"Go, Mom," Brynne instructed. "I'm coming. Don't worry about us."

Minutes were precious when it came to house fires. The average home went up in flames in three to four minutes, a staggering number. Don't get him started on all the synthetics and flammable materials inside of homes these days. There wasn't time.

"Pull your shirt up over your nose," he instructed, pointing toward hers and showing her to put it over her nose and mouth.

Brynne nodded as she coughed. She complied at the same time he pulled his up.

He reached for her hand and then linked their fingers as he headed toward the stairs. Brynne's room was at the top of the stairwell, which would make for a quick exit as long as the steps weren't on fire. Smoke thickened as they made their way down as quickly as their legs could carry them, making it impossible to see the bottom. Halfway down, he stopped. Flames licked the banister, and they were rising quickly. At this rate, the fire would meet them in the middle. They had to turn around and go back up.

The thought occurred to him someone might be using the fire to flush them out of the house. Or as a tactic to distract everyone. Maybe even cause enough confusion for them to split up again so the perp could snatch her a second time. *Not happening again, bastard.*

Did the sonofabitch want to finish the job he started? These moves went beyond jealousy. This was revenge. Someone felt scorned.

"Stick to me like a second skin," he said to Brynne as smoke chased them like a stalker in a dark alley. He led them back into her bedroom before closing the door to the hallway. She ran over to her dresser, opened a drawer and started tossing sweaters at him

"We can seal the bottom of the door with these," she said. Quick thinking on her part so opening the window didn't create a dangerous backdraft when he opened the window.

Fire crackled as it engulfed electrical appliances and climbed up the stairs like a rapid-growing vine.

He grabbed the quilted bedspread off the bed as she opened a window. Sounds of her mother screaming echoed through the complete blackness of the night, overpowering even the sizzle and mini explosions happening on the other side of the bedroom door. "Climb out the window and I'll lower you down first."

Brynne hesitated for a moment before taking in a deep breath and climbing out the window. Shrubbery below would catch her fall but also scratch her up. There was no time to do anything about it, so he clenched his back teeth and pushed ahead.

"Climb down," he said, gripping the comforter tightly and using his lower half to brace himself against the wall.

Brynne did as her mother came barreling around the corner, a desperate look on her face. She must have been expecting them to exit via the kitchen. Travis would have rather done that too, but here they were improvising. This was the way life worked. Plans were made. Plans were changed. He improvised.

Life was chaos and the trick was making adjustments on the fly.

Brynne's mother made a beeline underneath her daughter as she climbed down. The older woman pushed into the shrubs and helped buffer some of Brynne's fall. The two ended up tumbling onto the ground, Brynne's mother underneath.

A look of panic crossed Brynne's features as she immediately spun around to check on Travis. She grabbed her mother and rolled away from the downstairs window.

"Travis, wait!" she shouted a second before an explosion blew out the window. Flames licked the exterior of the home and filled the air.

Travis dove away from the window. He landed hard, slamming the back of his head on the dresser. He released a string of curses that would make his grandmother rise from her grave to wash his mouth out with soap.

Time was the enemy. He popped to his feet before moving back to the window. Shards of glass were sprinkled everywhere. Fire threatened to penetrate the door behind him in a matter of seconds.

It was now or never.

He climbed onto the window frame and jumped, trying to push out and away as far from the shrubs as humanly possible.

Travis landed wonky on his right ankle, tucked and rolled. He immediately popped to his feet and shook. Glass shards flew. He no doubt had a couple in his right shoulder, the shoulder he used to roll so he didn't break a body part.

"Are you okay?" Brynne's concern broke through while he took a physical inventory of the damage.

He picked two shards from his shoulder and then put pressure on the worst of the two to stem the bleeding. "I'm good."

"You're not," Brynne argued as she made her way over.

"I'm more concerned about you than I am a couple of cuts," he countered.

"Mom took the brunt of us falling," she explained. "She's okay, though. I might have broken a bone without her to soften my landing."

Thank the stars for small miracles. Travis pulled Brynne into an embrace. She leaned against his chest for the briefest moment, but the world righted itself.

They broke apart too soon for his liking, but they needed to get everyone away from the house. "Call your family over."

"Right after I call 911," Brynne stated. Good. She thought to grab her phone. His was still in his pocket too.

Right now, he needed to do his best to salvage the Beauden home. He grabbed the only thing he could find after bolting around to the back, a water hose.

"Fire," Brynne said into the phone as she and the others followed, which meant she got a dispatcher on the line. Good. It would still take the volunteer fire department a minimum of fifteen to twenty minutes to arrive. The house and its contents would be totally gone by then.

The older gentleman who'd introduced himself earlier as Saul Beauden grabbed a bucket. Again, it wouldn't do much but they had to do something to try to save the place.

"This shouldn't be happening," Brynne's grandmother said, her voice full of worry and stress. Guilt? It wouldn't surprise him.

After turning on the spigot to full blast, he took a few steps back and aimed at the structure. Jess Beauden went flying inside the back door.

"Stop," he demanded. She didn't. He doubted if she even heard him through the crackling fire that was now a full-on blaze. The winds weren't helping. Neither was the dry air.

Jess came out coughing with a red fire extinguisher in her hands. He had to hand it to her, she wanted to fight to keep her home. Brynne's mom disappeared around the side of the building before Travis could get her attention. No doubt, she was doing her part trying to stem some of the damage—damage that would claim her home and all her memories inside it.

The woman was losing control of her body, her business, and now her home. Bad news usually traveled in threes. Somehow, he thought it was just beginning for the Beaudens, rather than ending.

Whatever Travis could do to help when this was all over, he wouldn't hesitate. In fact, he fully intended to offer his family home while the farmhouse was rebuilt.

Jess came around with a renewed fierceness in her gaze. "I'm out, but I might have saved part of the structure with this." She held up the red extinguisher.

"No doubt," he reassured as he sprayed the back side of the home. He moved left, thinking the person who'd taken

Brynne before might have been trying to draw everyone out of the house. Why? Was there something inside they wanted?

No, that couldn't be right. They wouldn't set the place on fire if that was true. Would they? Not unless they believed they could get in and out without being detected.

He decided it would be too risky a move for anyone to pull off. Was this about destruction instead? Taking everything away from the Beaudens? This house meant independence to Jess and Brynne. Brynne had told him as much earlier. Losing it represented losing the life they'd built from nothing.

The sheriff came bolting out of the woods along with a deputy. He rushed over and got the lay of the land from Travis. Lawler shook his head as Jess plopped down on the grass and crossed her ankles. She gripped her knees and rocked back and forth.

Brynne squeezed Travis's shoulder before moving to her mother to comfort her. They were within ten feet of him, so he didn't stress about her leaving him. It wasn't far enough for him to worry.

He glanced over at the grandparents, who were huddled together. The grandmother, Rita, was softly crying. Saul comforted her. Both had that same look of guilt on their faces. He could see how much they'd been torturing themselves over their decision. They had a lot of work to do if they wanted Brynne to forgive them. In his heart of hearts, he knew she would rise to it if they were consistent. If they followed through on their intentions. But if they didn't, well, she was already done. She would walk away and never look back.

Rita held tightly to the pink knitting. It was bigger than a pot holder and years too late for a baby blanket for Brynne.

Then again, who was he to judge? Maybe it was some form of peace offering.

Sheriff Lawler stood sentinel over Brynne and her mother, which gave Travis room to breathe. The lawman seemed to realize Brynne was key to what was going on.

Travis joined them, still limping, as the first fire truck arrived. The cut on his shoulder stopped bleeding. He sat down on the grass across from Jess, next to Brynne. Instinctively, he reached for Brynne's hand and then linked their fingers. "How about staying at my house while yours is rebuilt?"

"Okay," Jess said, shocking him. He thought there would have to be some heavy convincing.

"It's close to here and it'll make it easier for you to supervise the rebuild," he explained. Over-explained might be a better word, since she'd already agreed.

"This is a sign," Jess said. "I'm selling."

"Hold on a red hot minute," Brynne protested. "Did you plan to discuss this with me first?"

"Of course, sweetheart," Jess said. "I just don't see how you can do everything on your own with a baby on the way." Jess's eyes widened as her shaky hand came up to cover her gasp.

"What makes you think I'm pregnant?" Brynne asked, shocked. But that word didn't nearly cover Travis's emotions. Because Brynne had admitted her relationship with Ty had been over a long time before she officially called it off. Which left one possibility for the father.

Him.

A look of panic crossed Brynne's features and she refused to make eye contact.

Why would she lie about something as important as a baby?

TRAVIS: Firebrand Cowboys 131

Since this wasn't the time or place to have the conversation brewing in his mind, he took in a deep breath and stood up. "I'll be over with the sheriff if you need me."

In his relatively short life, he'd learned when the time was right to dive into a problem and when to walk away to get some air. The decision was clear as day on this topic. Air.

Surprisingly, he was more hurt that Brynne hadn't told him about the baby—if her mom was right—than about becoming a father. The fact shocked the hell out of him.

∼

Brynne started to get up to follow Travis but stopped short. She'd had a few weeks now to adjust to the news and he'd found out in the worst possible way, her mom blurted it out without a workup or warning.

"What makes you think I'm pregnant?" Brynne asked her mother, once Travis was out of earshot. He needed time to adjust to the possibility and then he might be ready to hear the reason she hadn't told him yet. As far as her mother was concerned, on some level it was a relief the news was out. Hiding and keeping secrets was the worst feeling. Brynne had never been good at it. Not now. Not in high school when she'd skipped school but lied and said they had early release for a pep rally. And not before that in middle school when she hid her report card and said they didn't come out that day. In every instance, Brynne had come clean. She'd taken her punishments in stride, lucky they hadn't been harsh since she'd owned up to her lies.

"I'm still your mother, Brynne," her mom said. "You think I haven't noticed the changes in you? The morning sickness? The mood swings. The fact you stopped drinking coffee."

"I still drink coffee," she argued but the argument was hollow. The fight was drained from her for more reasons than one.

"You take the cup I give you for show," her mom said. "I looked out the kitchen window once and accidentally caught you pouring the contents of your cup into the hedges. I know you. You love your coffee. You wouldn't do that unless you had good reason."

"How long have you known?" Brynne asked, the fight drained from her. She'd never been good at covering up or withholding information. She'd never make a spy for a career. Luckily, farmers didn't have to worry about lying for a living.

Her mom shrugged. "Couple of weeks." She locked gazes with Brynne. "I thought the baby was Ty's. It's why I reached out to him. I knew the two of you were in a bad spot and I wanted to feel him out about the baby. See if he intended to keep up his end of the bargain."

It dawned on Brynne why her mom would interfere in her relationship. She'd been in a similar situation years ago with Brynne's father. She wanted Ty to step up.

"Did he say he was the father?" Brynne asked.

Her mom shook her head. "Didn't say he wasn't either. I just assumed we were on the same page but he blew up at me. I got confused about what we were fighting about and I couldn't, for the life of me, remember what I'd said that made him so upset. It's why I didn't tell you about him coming here."

Brynne exhaled. The news was out. Travis knew. There wasn't anything she could do about the fact now except hope he didn't hate her forever for not telling him sooner.

The expression on her mom's face nearly ripped Brynne to shreds. "I'm so sorry, Brynne. I've made a mess of things.

First with this stupid diagnosis and now with Travis. I thought I was helping and all I've done is destroy everyone around me."

"That's not true, Mom," Brynne argued. "You were the most amazing mother growing up and still are. You've been my best friend while we made it through tough times. This is no different. We're a team."

"I wasn't the best mother," her mom argued. "I couldn't be the mother I wanted to be. But you will. You will be there for your baby no matter what. Through thick and thin."

"How do you know that?" Brynne asked, unsure about everything when it came to parenting. "I don't have the first idea how to bring up a child. Let alone give this child a father."

"You love me," her mom said.

"That's not the same thing," Brynne pointed out.

"Unconditional love is rare, Brynne. It's what you give with no expectation of anything in return. It's your gift."

Brynne was shaking her head but her mom just took her hand to quiet her.

"You've weathered a lot of storms with me as your mom. That hasn't been easy. In some ways, I think you've brought me up more so than the other way around. You've been my north star when the darkness came crashing down around me. You're the reason I came back from it every time. Every time. Because eventually, your love would break through. Then, I would gather enough strength to sit up. Sitting up led to me being able to get into the shower. Showers eventually led me to getting out of bedclothes. Then, I would find enough energy to cook something."

A flood of tears rolled down Brynne's cheeks as her mom spoke.

"It was always you. I was able to fight my way back

because of you. And because of you, I'll keep fighting. I'll fight this disease until my last breath if it gives me more time with you and that baby of yours."

"I had no idea how hard it's been for you, Mom. Not until I started thinking about bringing up this little one on my own."

"You won't have to, Brynne. Your mom is going to be right here. And that's why it's time to sell the farm. This was my dream, not yours."

"That might be true," Brynne said. "But I can't think of a better legacy to leave to my own child someday, if they want it. And I want to keep this farm going." She needed to figure out how to rebuild the house and keep the business viable at the same time. But she had time before the baby arrived.

"You can't take care of the baby and me," her mom argued.

"Is that why you brought them back into our lives?" Brynne asked her mom as she glanced over at her crying grandmother as her grandfather tried to comfort her. They looked guilty as sin. Did they honestly want to change? Because she wouldn't have anyone calling her child a bastard. Not behind his or her back. Especially not to his or her face. And not while they were inside Brynne's home.

"Yes," her mom said. "At first, I reached out to tell them about the diagnosis."

"Why?"

"Because, honey, you never stop wanting your parents to love you," her mom admitted. "They may have turned their backs on me, but after we talked, I realized they suffered far more than we ever did. They missed your entire childhood and have no relationship with you now. Believe me when I say it's their loss. They realize it too."

Brynne glanced over at the pink knitting her grandmother was clinging to. "It's a little too late to make me a baby blanket, isn't it."

"That's not for you," her mom said. "It's for your baby. They're hoping for another girl. I think they're trying to make up for all that they missed with you."

Brynne guessed no one was all bad or all good.

"I still don't trust them," she said to her mom.

"They have a long way to go to earn your trust," her mom said. "And they know it, but people can change if we let them. Maybe they can make up for the past and be part of our lives. Help out when you have the baby and I can't do as much."

As though right on cue, they started toward Brynne and her mom. Brynne wasn't ready to forgive them. It might be because of the past, but she didn't trust them as far as she could throw them.

Saul spoke first as they approached. "We've made a terrible mistake."

You sure did.

Brynne must have given quite a look because her grandfather's face pinched.

"It's not what you think," he said with a frown.

"Then what?" Brynne asked.

"It's much worse," Saul said.

14

Travis tried to force the image of Brynne holding their newborn child in her arms from his thoughts. This wasn't the right time to fantasize about a future that was built on a betrayal.

He glanced over and saw Brynne's grandparents speaking to her, so he looked away.

"What do you make of all this, Sheriff?" he asked, refocusing on Lawler.

Sheriff Lawler issued a frustrated grunt. "The incident in the woods could have been a distraction." He shrugged. "This perp is always a step or two ahead. When we get close, he throws a curveball. None of the dots are connecting." He lifted his Stetson to rake his fingers through his hair. "This is the most frustrating point in any investigation when there are more questions than answers."

"We need a breakthrough," Travis agreed. "I offered my home for the family to stay in while theirs is rebuilt." He didn't regret the decision. Couldn't allow himself to. Regret was nothing more than a waste of time.

"They'll need a place now," the sheriff agreed.

Travis realized Brynne hadn't mentioned anything to the sheriff about the pregnancy either. Why?

It dawned on him. The baby was his and, therefore, she didn't see the information as relevant. However, since her mother knew about the baby and had had a dustup with Ty, Travis could only assume the guy was upset about her becoming pregnant at the time of their breakup. He might even believe she'd been cheating on him.

Brynne had mentioned Ty didn't take the breakup well. The man had a gambling addiction. The strikes against Ty were adding up. Could he also have been addicted to Brynne?

The sheriff needed to know this new information.

"What did your deputy say after interviewing the ex?" Travis asked the sheriff.

"He still hasn't been able to speak to him," Sheriff Lawler admitted. "The guy isn't answering his calls and he's not returning ours."

"The man has a gambling problem," Travis informed. "He might think the law is coming after him, since many forms of gambling are still illegal in Texas. My money says he isn't involved in the legal kinds."

"That very well could be true," Sheriff Lawler said.

"The crops," Travis began. "You were going to tell us about what you found from the aerial photos."

Sheriff Lawler nodded. "I found a Celtic knot known as the Trinity Knot."

"Like the Holy Trinity?" Travis asked, confused as to how that might apply to Brynne and her mother or their farm.

"That's what I thought too until I looked up the meaning," Lawler confided. "It's often the symbol couples in Ireland exchange in jewelry to show love and devotion. At least, that's what Google said."

"Which points the finger directly at Ty, am I right?" Travis asked.

"Or back to you," the sheriff said. "But we know that's not the case since someone almost got away with abducting Brynne."

From the corner of Travis's eye, he saw Brynne making a beeline toward the two of them with her grandparents in tow. The look on her face stirred up a hornet's nest of questions.

"Sheriff," she said before risking a glance over at Travis. He looked away, unwilling and unable to make eye contact at this point. "These people have something to tell you."

Saul stepped forward first. His wife practically hid behind him. "We're the ones responsible for all this." He waved his hand around.

"Excuse me?" Sheriff Lawler asked, not hiding his shock.

"You have to understand, we'd just learned about our daughter's condition," Saul began, looking like a kid who'd stolen a brownie out of the cookie jar instead of a man who'd caused this much damage and pain.

The sheriff's eyebrows drew together. "I'm afraid I'm not following."

Brynne caught her mom's gaze. Jess gave a slight nod.

"My mother has been diagnosed with Parkinson's disease," Brynne stated, wrapping an arm around her mother for support. "She's been dealing with the diagnosis on her own, not quite ready to share the news with the whole town." Brynne stared at the sheriff. "You know how folks can be with gossip."

"Yes, ma'am," he said. "I'm afraid I do."

"Then, hopefully you can understand why my mom needed to get her arms around this diagnosis before word spread and she was flooded with questions," Brynne continued. "Even well-meaning folks can make a situation worse when you're not prepared, and this has been keeping my mom up nights as it is."

"I do understand," Sheriff Lawler said before turning to Brynne's mother. "I'm sorry to hear about this, Ms. Beauden. I hope you know that my deputies and I are here to help in any way we can."

"Much appreciated, Sheriff," Jess said with a look of relief. Some of the tension in her facial muscles eased. Was she relieved word was finally out?

"She told my grand...*her parents*...about the diagnosis and they decided, without consulting anyone, mind you, that she needed to sell the farm," Brynne continued. "They told her it was the only way. She could sell the farm and then move in with them. The money from the proceeds would be enough to take care of her for many years to come."

The logic sounded reasonable to Travis, except that he knew how much pride Jess and Brynne had in their small farm.

"They also convinced her not to say anything to me about the plan because, I guess, they believed I wouldn't have it," she said. "Said I was too proud to admit defeat and that I would end up running the farm into the ground and we'd be penniless."

"We thought we were doing what was right," Saul stated.

"Doing something right?" Brynne repeated, her face red with anger. She sucked in a breath. "There's another complication that I haven't told you about." This time, Travis glanced up and met eyes that were studying him. "I'm pregnant. My mom figured it out and confided in her parents. Parents, she believed, finally had her best interests at heart. And mine."

Sheriff Lawler's eyes widened. Dots were beginning to connect in his brain the same way they were in Travis's. Travis could see it in the lawman's eyes.

"You would think at this point, someone would clue me in to all this backroom chatter, but they didn't," Brynne continued. "Instead, this man here." She pointed a finger at Saul. "Decided I would sell in a heartbeat if I was pregnant and scared. So, he hired someone to make the crop circles and splash animal blood on the site."

Travis's heartbeat was pounding the inside of his ribcage at this point. Anger? Check. More anger? Check. Angrier than he'd ever been? Check.

"You had someone kill one of my calves and then abduct your own granddaughter in the name of caring?" This sounded like some kind of twisted nonsense his family would pull.

"Not abducted," Saul immediately said. "That was never part of the deal."

"Who did you hire to make the crop circles?" Travis asked, figuring the name would lead them to the bastard who'd crossed the line.

"Santiago," Saul said. "He was in hard financial straits so we helped him out."

"*Targeted* is more like it," Brynne practically hissed. "Didn't you think the sheriff would investigate everyone who worked here? He would find the bank deposits."

"Santiago was instructed to wait thirty days to deposit the money," Saul said. "After all this blew over."

"That's rich," Brynne huffed. "You abused someone who is down on his luck to get what you wanted, all without telling your daughter."

"She gets confused," Saul said by way of explanation as if that justified their actions. "And we didn't want her to be implicated. What she didn't know couldn't be used against her."

"You make me sick," Brynne said to Saul. "I honestly can't understand how you could be so manipulative. Do you think the world is waiting around for your approval? For you to step in and save us? You turned your back on me the day I was born. Before I was even born you turned your back on your daughter. And now, you've crossed a criminal line."

"Is the buyer already set up?" Jess asked, much to her father's horror.

"What do you mean?" Saul asked, playing innocent.

"I was in the bathroom while you made calls," Jess said. "Do you really think the walls are made of concrete?"

"Perfect," Brynne said sarcastically. "I'm guessing you had a great price already in mind."

"Times have been hard on us too," Saul continued, shoulders rounded forward.

Before Brynne could explode with rage, Travis took a step toward her in the hopes of calming her down. He reached for her hand and linked their fingers. Caught her gaze.

"We're taking a walk," he said to the small gathering without breaking eye contact. The sheriff would arrest Saul and Rita. Justice would be served for their part in this. But there was still someone out there who wanted Brynne. It wasn't the same person who'd drawn the crop circles. Unless she was being set up for ransom.

He shook it off as he studied Brynne, hoping she would go with him. She gave a slight nod, which he took as a green light to keep walking.

Once they were out of earshot, he stopped and turned

toward her. "All this stress can't be good for you or the baby."

"Lizzy, my OB, said the fetus might not even take," Brynne said. "It's why I didn't say anything no matter how much I wanted to."

"What does that mean?"

"A lot of pregnancies don't make it to the second trimester," she explained, practically heaving for air as she spoke. Nerves? Stress? All of the above?

"Hey," he said to her, wishing he could find the words to calm her down.

Instead, she continued, "I'm so sorry I didn't say anything before. There's no excuse for keeping this news from you, except that I didn't want you to go through all this...stress...if you didn't have to. Once the pregnancy was in the clear, I planned to show up at your door. I just didn't want to work you up over nothing if things didn't work out."

The logic made sense, even though his emotions were running the show right now.

"We can discuss all that later," he said. "Right now, I'm worried about you. All this stress isn't good for you, and I've never felt more helpless when it comes to helping you."

"You don't hate me?" she immediately asked.

"No," he said without thinking. He didn't need to think to answer her question. Baby or not, he didn't hate her. On some level, he could see that she'd been in a difficult situation. One he could understand there were layers to. If he wasn't on the receiving end of the pregnancy news, he would probably have advised her to do the same thing if she'd come to him.

He couldn't fault her for doing the best she could, and it certainly wasn't her fault she'd gotten pregnant. Last he checked, it took two to tango. And it had been one helluva tango that weekend.

But he was getting off track, and he didn't need the reminder of how easy it was to fall for Brynne. Or did he?

~

He didn't hate her.

There were no words for the amount of relief Brynne felt in the revelation.

She finally exhaled the breath it felt like she'd been holding for months. Travis knew. Her mother knew. Now, the sheriff knew.

Ty knew too, a little voice in the back of her mind pointed out.

"You think he's responsible, don't you?" she asked. They both knew who she was talking about so there was no point in saying his name.

"I thought he was the one who did all of it," Travis admitted. "But I wondered what the crop circle had to do with getting back at you."

"To scare me," she guessed. "Maybe he thought I would come running back to him if I was scared."

"It makes sense, but now we know there were two entities at work," he said as he explained the Celtic knot found in the aerial photos. "Your grandfather has admitted to being one of them."

"He's not my relation," she quipped. "I'll find a way to forgive them and find peace for my sake, not theirs. They tried to manipulate my mom too. I was starting to consider forgiving them for the past but they haven't changed. They intended to profit off something my mom and I built together. They had no hand in the farm's success but everyone is right about one thing."

He cocked an eyebrow.

"I can't do everything," she admitted. It pained her to say those words but they were true. "I'm only one person. My mom is going to need more support than ever. I'll have to take on extra responsibilities at the farm." She glanced down at her stomach. "This little bean is going to need me, if we get the green light in a couple of weeks."

"You don't have to do this alone, Brynne."

Now, it was Brynne's turn to be confused.

"I'm here, Brynne. I'm not going anywhere, and I'm certainly not turning my back on my child. You'll have all the resources you need to care for the kid and I'd like to be involved on a daily basis."

"I appreciate that, Travis. Believe me when I say that I know what it's like to have a parent give up on you before you're even born. This child, should that be the case, deserves to have both parents involved in its life. But I know you need time to process all this. It's a lot."

"Not as much as I thought it would be," he stated, surprising the hell out of her. It was clear that she hadn't given him nearly enough credit for the incredible human being he was. "I could never turn my back on my own flesh and blood. The circumstances don't matter. Besides, it's not like you made this child alone. You shouldn't have to raise it that way."

Brynne had had a gut feeling Travis would want to be involved once he got over the shock of the news. She'd had no idea what that might look like, though, and had been certain he would resent her because she knew Ty would have reacted that way. Travis and Ty couldn't be more opposite.

"We can talk about visitation and financial support once we're clear of all this. You should know that I plan to take care of this child and you financially, so you'll never have to work again if you don't want to. Right now, you have a stalker on your back that's been one step ahead of us," Travis explained. "The deputy never reached your ex, by the way."

"Which could mean he's around here somewhere right now," she surmised. The dead calf made sense, if Ty had put two-and-two together about Travis. But she still didn't know how her ex would have figured out Travis was the child's father.

A lot was about to change in her life. She had ideas about making some changes to the farm once this was behind her too.

"Does your offer to stay at your place at Firebrand still stand?" she asked, not taking anything for granted. "Because I would understand if it didn't under the circumstances. I know you didn't ask for any of this."

"I wouldn't go back on an offer like that," he said indignantly. She hadn't meant to offend him, only give him a way out in case he regretted the decision. "Of course, it still stands."

"I appreciate everything you're willing to do for my mom and me," she said with the first hint of a real smile in longer than she cared to admit. The news was out. Soon, everyone in town would know too. Would they make comments *like mother, like daughter*?

Strangely, she didn't care as much as she thought she would. Now that Travis knew and didn't hate her, no one else mattered. If she'd known telling him sooner would have brought this much relief, she would have done it immediately. Walking around like you held a ticking time bomb that might destroy someone's life had been a heavy burden to bear. Here she'd thought she was sneaky, but her mom figured it out even in her anxious state.

"Are we good?" Travis asked, studying her.

"I'm so good, Travis."

"Are you calm?" he asked.

"Better than before," she reassured.

"Good because all this stress isn't good for you or the kid," he said and then surprised her by reaching for her hand. He linked their fingers and his touch brought a wave of warmth washing over her.

Could she trust it?

15

Travis scanned the area as the firefighters put out the last of the fire. He reached into his pocket for his cell phone to make a few calls. Clean-up would be expensive, and he wanted to salvage what memories he could for Brynne and her mom. Losing pictures and keepsakes had to be the worst part of a devastating loss like this one.

He fired off a few texts to get the clean-up crew rolling, while Jess got on the phone with her insurance agent.

Sheriff Lawler was the conductor in this chaotic orchestra, but everything was getting done. Statements were given. Arrests were made.

Travis thought about the kid he had on the way and about how becoming a father might change him. He figured it might require adjustments on all levels of his life, which should scare the hell out of him.

The little voice in the back of his head that was good at pointing out things he didn't always want to hear was dead on when it said, *Maybe it's time for a change.*

Life as he'd known it so far had been spinning out of

control for what felt like an eternity, but was really the past year. Why did *this* make sense? Why did being with Brynne make sense?

Could they try a relationship and see where it led?

The short answer was that they couldn't afford to mess up with a baby on the way. Despite the feelings he had for Brynne, acting on them would be a mistake. Because what would happen when the relationship ended and they had to force themselves to get along for the sake of a kid?

Travis had grown up with parents who didn't love each other. At least, on the surface it seemed that way. His mother had been a trophy wife who came from an abusive household. Would history repeat itself?

Hell no.

There was no way Travis would ever hurt his kid and neither would Brynne. He'd seen it in the way she cradled her stomach during stressful times, which now made sense why she'd done it. She'd caught herself a few times and corrected her reach, bringing an awkward hand up to tuck a piece of hair behind her ear. So much about her behavior up to this point was clear to him now. He'd chalked it up to stress but now he knew different.

He turned to her as she stood next to him. She'd been on her feet all day in stressful conditions.

"Maybe we should call your doctor," he said to Brynne. "Just to be safe."

"I talked to Lizzy when I last took a shower," Brynne admitted. "Sneaked a phone call in when I went upstairs first. She said as long as there's no cramping or bleeding I should be fine."

"And if there is?"

"I should call her immediately," she supplied.

"All the smoke from the fire isn't something you should

be breathing in," he continued, realizing just how many carcinogens there were in housefires.

Brynne smiled even though it didn't reach her eyes. "I've been worried about how you would take the news if, in fact, I ended up being in the position to need to deliver it. I thought you would hate me for the rest of our lives. Seeing you be so concerned..."

She tucked her chin to her chest and looked away. Was she crying?

Discreetly, she brought her hand up to wipe what had to be a stray tear.

"I'm here, Brynne," he reassured. "I'm not going anywhere. Over the next however many months, I plan to do everything I can to make this easier on you."

Establishing trust was the foundation of co-parenting. He was convinced of the fact. If Brynne knew she could count on him, she could relax. At least, that was the hope. He wanted a healthy mother and baby. So, yeah, his job from now on was going to be protecting and supporting Brynne.

And then he planned to step up and be a real father. Not the absent kind, like his old man had been. But one who showed up for the kid. Parent-teacher conferences? He planned to be at every single one. Sports practices? He'd do his best to make all those. Games? Yes. And if this was a girl, he'd show up to dance class if that was what made her heart sing.

He'd had a front-row view of bad parenting. Flip everything they did, or even more importantly, didn't do, and he had a roadmap to being a good parent. Funny how that worked. Maybe he should thank them, after all.

∼

Emotions had been on a roller coaster ride ever since finding out about her mom's diagnosis and then the pregnancy. This was the first time in weeks Brynne actually saw a ray of hope in her situation.

"Thank you, Travis," she started. "For taking the news so well. And for planning to step up. Believe me when I say not everyone does." Her own father came to mind. And then her grandparents, who'd turned out to be even bigger disappointments than she'd originally believed them to be, which was saying a whole lot.

"Don't thank me yet," Travis said with a cocky half-grin. "I'm just getting started."

"Should I be scared?" she teased, appreciating the break in tension.

"Yes, very," he quipped. "But right now, I just want to get you out of here and into a safer environment. I want to take you home." He caught himself. "To my home where you and your mom can get comfortable and rest, and we can put this behind us and start picking up the pieces again."

"Okay," she said. "I'll just grab her and we can head out. I already gave my statement to the sheriff, but I'll make sure it's okay to leave."

On the walk over, Brynne had a thought about the buyer her grandparents had lined up. Could that be the reason things have gone too far? If they hired Santiago to scare her, maybe a potential buyer thought they could get the place at an even bigger discount if Brynne and her mom were scared to come back.

Anything was possible.

She detoured over to the sheriff and asked the question on her mind.

"They are saying they don't have a buyer yet," Sheriff Lawler said, making a face.

"Do you believe them?" she asked.

"Not as far as I can throw them right now," he admitted. "That could also be because I can't imagine anyone who would sell out their family this way."

"They did nothing to make the farm a success," she added. "It's wrong on so many levels that they want to profit from all of our work at this point. Don't even get me started on cutting me out of the picture when I'm the one who helped build this place to what it is."

Greed made sense, though. Wasn't it one of the top motives for murder? If memory served, she'd read the statistic somewhere or heard it on the news.

"What will happen to Santiago?" she asked. What he'd done was wrong. There was no doubt about it. But if he went to jail, his mother and child would receive no support, which didn't seem fair. Her grandparents had taken advantage of a desperate man.

"That partially depends on you," Sheriff Lawler said.

"How so?"

"Do you want to press charges against him?" Sheriff Lawler asked.

"I have a choice?" she asked.

"This is private property and he works for you," he stated. "As far as I know the crop circle was a prank that was taken too far. While one of my deputies tried to locate him, he was showing up at my office to turn himself in. There's no way he was the one who attempted to abduct you."

"He wouldn't take it that far," she agreed. "Not the Santiago I know."

"He's asking to speak to you and your mother directly," the sheriff said. "Wants to apologize personally."

"Okay," she said. "I'll agree to hear him out before I press charges."

"He isn't trying to get out of going to jail," Sheriff Lawler informed. "Said he doesn't deserve to walk around free after scaring you the way he did but he also said he's not responsible for the blood."

"Do you believe him?" she asked.

"Yes," the sheriff said.

"What he did was wrong," she reasoned. "There's no denying that." She paused a couple of beats, gathering her thoughts. "However, he was manipulated into it and since you believe the blood wasn't his doing, he really only damaged some of the crop. Is it possible for him to get a slap on the wrists instead of going to court?"

"I can have a talk with him and let him know if he so much as jaywalks he'll go to jail if that would help," Sheriff Lawler offered.

"Do you think I'm doing the right thing in not pressing charges?" she asked.

"Santiago has been part of this community for a long time," the sheriff reasoned. "He's been a good father who has done his best to keep up his child support payments, even when it meant going to bed hungry, according to his mother. Sometimes, folks deserve a second chance."

She nodded. "I have an idea of how he can earn a better living."

The sheriff cocked an eyebrow.

"The folks doing the work building the farm should profit from it too," she said, matter of fact. "I think the best move will be to offer profit sharing to the handful of folks who've come back year after year." She glanced down at her stomach. "There's no way Mom and I can handle running this place alone, not with everything on our plates. The farm wouldn't be where it is today without Hector, Santiago, and a couple more of the men who've come back season after season. Making them partners only makes sense and is a better legacy than forcing the family business solely on any children I might have. With me to lead the office side of the business, Mom will be able to step back even more when the time comes. I can hire someone to work in the office if we ramp up production. We'll figure it all out. And then I'll have time for other..." She glanced down at her belly. "Pursuits."

With Travis's financial support, she could work less at the farm and help it grow.

Could she resurrect her art career on the side?

"The Turners did the same thing five years ago," The sheriff supplied. "Said they couldn't imagine why they'd waited so long. If you have questions, they'll be able to help out with answers."

"Thanks," she said. "I better get back to Travis and my mom."

"That's all I need," he said. "I'll be around a few more minutes out front if anything comes up.

Brynne thanked the sheriff one more time before heading over to her mom and Travis. She never thought she'd see the day when her mom got along with a Firebrand. Life was changing, and it was about time.

Besides, she wanted her mom to have a good relationship with the father of her child. If this pregnancy worked out, the families would be spending time around each other. She wanted the baby to grow up in an atmosphere filled with love and with a family bigger than Brynne and her mom. Thankfully, Travis seemed on board.

There were so many other Firebrands. The bean would grow up with more cousins than Brynne could imagine. She'd been an only child. The same as her mother had been. Based on what she'd seen so far, the Firebrand brothers and cousins had all turned out to be good people, despite their messed up upbringing. It gave her hope that her grandparents wouldn't rub off on the little bean, not that Brynne planned to have anything to do with the older couple after what they'd pulled.

"I almost forgot, I need to tell the sheriff something," she said to Travis, who'd reached for her hand.

Travis glanced around the backyard. "I'll go with you."

"No, stay with Mom while she's being cleared," she said as an EMT shined a small light in her mother's eyes. "Sheriff Lawler is out front and I want to ask him to keep Mom's diagnosis to himself for the time being and ask him if he thinks her parents might be convinced to do the same." She shivered from the cold that was settling in.

"Take this," Travis said, taking off his flannel shirt and wrapping it around her shoulders.

"You'll freeze," she pointed out, shaking her head.

It was too late. Travis had made up his mind. Much to her surprise, she didn't mind being spoiled a little bit after going the past few months on her own with no one to talk to about the pregnancy or her mom's condition.

"I'll be fine," her mom protested.

"That may be, but Travis will bring you around front if I'm not back in a couple of minutes," she said.

"Hollar if you need me," Travis said, catching her gaze.

Even that simple act of looking her in the eyes sent warmth rolling through her. For the first time in a very long time, she believed things might work out alright. Did she want more than that from Travis?

Yes.

Would she risk hurting their tentative friendship and possibly make life uncomfortable for their child to act on an attraction, no matter how intense?

No.

So, she headed around the house.

"Meow," came the little voice.

Brynne spun around to see the little tabby heading straight toward her. She dropped down onto her knees as relief washed over her. "Sweet girl, you're alive." Tears sprang to her eyes. Tears of relief. Tears of joy. Tears for the tabby who was alive. "You need a name."

The ruckus around the house, along with the fire, must have brought her out of hiding, searching for a safe place.

"Meow." She drew out the sound this time like she was lodging a complaint about the noises or, the smoke, or all of the above.

The little cat did something she never used to, she lay down in front of Brynne.

"Hey, how does this feel, Tabitha?" Brynne asked, scratching her behind the ears, thinking she'd found the perfect name for the tabby.

The little yellow tabby batted at Brynne's fingers and meowed again, louder this time.

"Oh, you want a belly rub?" Brynne asked as she moved her hands over the little tabby's chest, scratching while making soothing sounds. She probably looked ridiculous but didn't care. "I thought I lost you."

A few more rogue tears slipped out of the corners of Brynne's eyes. Was this a sign life was finally turning around after beating Brynne and her mother up for months?

If it was, she couldn't think of a better one.

"I'll be back, Tabitha," she said to the newly-named tabby. She wanted to catch the sheriff before he took off.

Tabitha stood up and wound through Brynne's ankles.

Times were changing, looking up.

Brynne couldn't help but smile despite the only home

she'd ever known being all but destroyed. She's shared this home with her mom for her entire life. Dreams of going away to college had been dashed in order to keep the family business going. But she had a plan to keep the legacy alive while giving space to grow away from it. The feeling of pride had her practically floating around the burnt building.

As she rounded the corner to where the sheriff's vehicle had been parked, a hand grabbed her and pulled her close. Another hand came over her mouth, stifling her voice and her ability to scream.

This time, she recognized the perp despite the EMT shirt...Ty.

16

A frantic guy, looked to be mid-twenties, came into view from the tree line. Shirtless, he waved his arms in the universal sign for help as he came running toward Travis.

Travis met him halfway. A few steps into the run, he realized this was the new EMT from Houston by the name of Eric. Eric worked out at the gym but that wasn't the only thing Travis noticed about the guy. There was blood on his face and chest.

"I got jumped," Eric said. "There was someone in the woods who called me over, saying he needed help. He was on the ground and I assumed he was part of whoever had been in the house. His face was dirty with what looked like soot, which made me believe he'd been inside." This close, it was obvious someone had broken Eric's nose. "I thought maybe he'd become disoriented and wandered outside and into the trees."

All the blood rushed from Travis's face. He didn't need a mirror to realize what was happening. He felt it with a whoosh. *Brynne.*

He immediately turned and scanned the area. There was no sign of her, but he couldn't see the front of the home or the parking pad from this vantage point.

"Did you get a good look at the person who did this to you?" he asked Eric.

"He was about yay tall," Eric started, holding his hand up to around the tip of Travis's nose. Since he was six-feet-four-inches, he assumed the guy they were looking for was five-feet-eleven-inches, give or take. "And decently strong."

"Face description?" Travis asked, realizing he was losing valuable time standing here talking to Eric. Thankfully, Brynne was with the sheriff.

Still, he'd feel a whole lot better if he could see her with his own eyes right now. A feeling deep in the pit of his stomach said something wasn't right. It was probably him being paranoid but he needed to see Brynne to calm himself down.

Right now, all of his muscles tensed and a knot fisted inside his chest.

"He motioned for me to bend down and when I did, he threw a punch that knocked me out," Eric admitted. He wasn't that tall, but he must be strong. The person who got the drop on him had to be strong enough to throw a knockout punch.

"I'm guessing you have no idea where he went next," Travis said, skimming the tree line. Not that it did any good in the dark. The area around the house was still lit by fire trucks and headlights. The barn was far enough away from the main house not to have received damage. The light was still on.

Eric shook his head.

Whoever was responsible for killing a calf had to be the same person who set the house on fire. The bastard was causing chaos, flushing them out into the open where it would be easier to snatch Brynne.

More of that panic slammed into Travis. He wasn't able to protect Brynne in the woods. The guy outsmarted Travis. He flexed and released his fingers a couple of times to release some of the tension at the thought.

"I'm gonna head over and get checked out," Eirc said, motioning toward where Jess sat, leaning up against a tree trunk. Jess had lost her home. She was losing her health. The woman had lost so much.

Travis held his own hands up, palms flat. Every day, he took for granted they would work when he needed them to. They picked up objects, held forks so he could eat. He couldn't imagine how awful it would feel not to be able to rely on them.

The unsettled feeling in the pit of his stomach grew. In order to calm down, he needed to see Brynne. He needed to know she was fine and still with the sheriff.

Heading around the front of the house, walking around the devastation, careful not to step on anything sharp that might drill a hole through his boot, he picked up the pace. The need to see Brynne grew with every step forward.

Suddenly, the pregnancy didn't matter. The fact she'd kept it from him didn't matter. The deception didn't matter.

Nothing mattered except finding her and seeing that she was okay with his own eyes.

The blood-curdling scream he heard caused his heart to skip a few beats.

Travis bolted toward the sound, scared to death he would miss her again, and this time the bastard would win.

He rounded the corner of the house to realize the sheriff was gone. The fire truck's lights swirled but there was no one in the vicinity. They were all around the back of the house with the EMTs and Jess.

In Brynne's Chevy, though, there was a fight.

Brynne was fighting for her life.

Travis grabbed the door handle and then pulled the door open. He yanked the bastard wearing an EMT shirt off of Brynne. The dude looked surprised as he was tossed to the ground. "Are you hurt?"

"I'm alright," Brynne said, gasping for air. "I'll be okay. Don't let Ty get away."

This jerkoff was damn desperate if he was willing to yank Brynne away from this scene, with Travis there as well as other strong men.

Ty was scrambling to his feet, reaching for something inside his pant leg. A gun? A knife?

Travis dove on top of Ty, pinning him to the ground. "Call the sheriff. He has one more to pick up."

Those words didn't sit well with Ty. He bucked and grunted, but his strength was no match for Travis. He wrestled for control of the metal object in Ty's hand. Received a slice from a sharp blade, realized it was a knife.

Rather than go for the blade, Travis went for Ty's wrist to stop him from jabbing Travis. With both hands wrapped around the guy's wrists, Travis brought a knee up to jab Ty's thigh.

Ty groaned in pain and bit out a few choice words.

"You might as well get used to it," Travis said. "I don't think people will show you a whole lot of mercy where you're going." He thought about the fight his own mother had been in, a fight that hadn't been her fault.

As Ty struggled, help arrived in the form of EMTs and firefighters.

The dude was overwhelmed in two minutes flat. Travis

gripped the knife, forcing it out of Ty's hand, checked his own wound. The cut wasn't terrible. Travis would be fine.

"That bitch owes me," Ty spit out. "She's been bad, and she owes me a future. She'll see, once I get her back home that we're meant for each other. She never should have walked out on me. She'll come around. What we have is eternal."

"No, thanks," Brynne said to him as he was being held down. He tried to spit at her. "You've fallen down a dark hole, Ty. Someday, I hope you can pull yourself out of it. There used to be a decent person in there. Either way, I never want to see you again for as long as I live."

Travis could only hope the opposite was true about him. Because he had something to say, and he didn't care who heard him say it.

～

BRYNNE SAT on the bench seat of the Chevy that had been with her through a whole lot over the years. Travis moved to her as sirens split the air in the distance.

He took her hand in his and then took a knee in front of her.

"Brynne, I've been a fool not to tell you this sooner," he started. "But the thought of losing you did things to me...to my heart. And I've come to the realization that I want you in my life as a permanent fixture."

Her heart swelled at those words.

"My timing is probably off once again, just like it was two months ago, but I'm happy about the baby and I'd like to be more than co-parents," he continued, looking straight through her with those beautiful eyes of his. "I'd like to ask you to marry me when you're ready. *If* you ever become ready. Because I'm in love with you and I can't imagine spending another minute without you in my arms and in a home we built together."

He smiled. His eyes were full of vulnerability despite the fact he was the strongest person she knew.

"So, what do you say?" he asked. "Move in with me? Marry me at some point. I don't care when. I'd like to take care of you during the pregnancy and make sure you have everything you need. Will you let me?"

He stopped right there. The sincerity in his eyes caused her chest to squeeze.

"How do you feel about having a mother-in-law who lives with you full-time?" Brynne asked with half a smile. She could do this. She could see herself living with Travis for the rest of her life, happy as a lark.

"Jess became family the minute this little bean was formed," he said.

"Good," Brynne said. "Because I've loved you since middle school. Probably further back than that. I was wildly in love with you in high school and just didn't know it. And now? I'm heart-all-in with you, Travis. I can't imagine ever meeting anyone who makes me feel the way you do." She reached down with her free hand and cradled her stomach. "I can't imagine having a better father for this baby or a better partner for the rest of my life. Plus, you're all kinds of hot."

She felt her cheeks flush but didn't care. He was hot and he should know it.

"I'll move in with you," she said. "I'll marry you. I'll have this family with you. Because I love you. But I want to keep a hand on the farm too. My mom and I built this legacy together and I want to stay involved."

"You can have anything you want," he said to her. "As long as you come home to me at the end of every day."

Travis stood up, looped his arms around her, and then dipped his head down and kissed her. His lips were so tender that the kiss robbed her breath.

"I have a condition of my own, though," he informed as his face morphed to serious.

"Okay," she said, drawing out the word. There wasn't much she wouldn't do for the man as long as she could maintain her independence.

"We build an art studio behind the cabin and here during the rebuild so you can get back to doing what you've always loved," he said.

For the first time, Brynne couldn't wait to see what tomorrow held. And she couldn't wait to face the future with Travis.

"You drive a hard bargain, Firebrand," she said with a smile that she felt in her whole body. "But my answer is yes. It will always be yes."

With that, Travis kissed her again, slow and tender, marking her as his. And she couldn't be happier.

17

EPILOGUE

Kellan Firebrand tapped this thumb on the steering wheel of his pickup, sitting in the gravel driveway of his cabin. His attempts to reach his brother Travis by cell had been fruitless so far. Rumor had it that his brother was wounded in a knife fight. Kellan needed to see with his own two eyes that his brother was fine. After everything that had gone down since the Marshal's death, Kellan left nothing to chance. Besides, he'd been needing to talk to someone and Travis was levelheaded. He would give sound advice.

A visit to his brother's house could kill two birds with one stone. Or, at least, that was the logic. Should he call first? Or show up unannounced?

Was Kellan ready to talk or would he back out again before making the trip? For the couple of times he'd attempted to call his brother, there were a half dozen where he couldn't make his finger tap Travis's name in his contacts.

Kellan had information that directly impacted his brother. The question was whether or not Travis could handle the news, if it was true. Kellan was ninety-nine percent certain it was. But that one percent chance it wasn't, haunted him.

The truck windows were down. The sun setting. The sky was the real prize of living in Texas, nothing but powder blue for miles and miles tonight. Kellan loved the sky, the land and that was about all. He'd lived in Lone Star Pass his entire life, didn't know any different.

Divorced, family in turmoil, and a year and a half shy of his fortieth birthday, Kellan played around with the idea of pulling up roots and getting the hell out of Dodge. Not just Lone Star Pass. For the first time in his life, he wondered what it would be like to start fresh in a new state.

The thumb tapping intensified.

Windows down, a breeze swept through the truck.

At this point, he couldn't see that he had anything to lose if he jumped ship. What exactly did he have to keep him here? Rumor had it Travis was planning to get married, making Kellan the lone holdout.

The tension between him and his cousin Adam, despite attempting to make peace for the family's sake, was worse than ever and getting old. Kellan tried to warm up to the other side of the family, but a lifetime spent standing on opposite sides of just about every issue took its toll.

Then there was the whole town of Lone Star Pass that was against Kellan's side of the family tree. People stared when he went into town to grab supplies that couldn't be ordered or delivered. His mother's actions had made matters worse. Carrying the last name Firebrand was a curse.

To add insult to injury, Adam's side of the family had moved into and taken over the Marshal's house almost immediately after the old man's death. According to his will, they had every right. But had any one of those so-called 'good Firebrands' sat any member of his side of the family down and asked if that was okay?

Nope. Not once.

Kellan had been playing along with making amends for his brothers' sake. The charade, swallowing his words, holding back was like a volcano waiting to erupt inside his chest. He was about to blow. Would it make everything worse?

Should he drive over to his brother's or call? Travis might not be home.

Then again, his brother's cabin was on the property. It wouldn't take more than half an hour to make the drive. He picked up his cell, pulled up Travis's name, and tapped the screen to make the call.

It rolled into voicemail.

"Hey, I was hoping to catch you. We need to talk. *I* need to talk, but—"

The call dropped, cutting the connection. Kellan bit back a curse. Of course, it did. Would his brother get the message or would the phone mess that up too? It happened. He'd make a call, expect a callback, only to find out the person on the receiving end never got the message. They weren't lying about it, either. These fancy phones weren't as reliable as they should be for how much they cost.

A crash in his equipment room shocked him out of his reverie. It was probably that damn raccoon again. He set the phone down in the cupholder to investigate. The last time a raccoon visited, the darn thing chewed an electrical cord, which could have started a fire, and chewed through a wall before leaving behind 'presents' inside the wall that stunk to high heaven.

Kellan didn't need the hassle, but Murphy's Law said more bad luck was on the way.

He banged on the door as he fished a set of keys out of his jeans pocket. "Get out of my shed." Although, *shed*, wasn't nearly fancy enough of a word for his equipment room. Considering his cabin was a one-bedroom, he didn't have a whole of storage. One side of this space kept anything that didn't fit inside his house, and the other half kept equipment and tools.

Inside the shed, it was quiet. That was odd. Normally, the raccoon scurried around when he shouted. He'd hear its nails against the tile. Was this flooring fancy for an equipment shed? Yes. But it was built well to keep vermin out. Usually.

Raccoons were demons with fur.

He jangled the keys. Startling a wild animal that might perceive itself as being cornered was responsible for the six-inch scar that ran across his chest. He'd learned the lesson as a teen when common sense had taken a vacation and he'd cornered a coyote. Needless to say, the coyote won.

Kellan slowly opened the door, banging it with the set of keys. If the raccoon saw his or her exit, it would most likely escape.

There was nothing, not a sound.

Kellan stepped inside as he flicked on the overhead light. Damn raccoon must have chewed the chord because nothing happened. He muttered a string of choice words under his breath. Shelves on the righthand side of the room held several varieties of flashlights and battery-operated camping lamps.

He'd made a trail through the middle of the room the last time he was in here looking for wire cutters, shoving chairs and stacking cabinets to the side. Murphy's Law kicked in again because that was the side of the room he needed to get to in order to have light.

It dawned on him that the cell phone in his pocket had a flashlight app feature. And then he immediately realized he'd left the phone inside his truck.

There was very little daylight to draw on at this point, so the opened door did him no good. There was also a window to his right but he'd pushed a dresser up against that side.

Taking a step, he immediately drew his foot back. The shot he'd taken to the shin hurt like hell. What was in the way?

He bent down to feel around as the door to the shed closed behind him. He heard the latch close, essentially locking him in.

The lock wouldn't be able to do that on its own. Someone had to be out there.

"Hey!" Kellan turned and hopped over to the door on his good leg, slamming his fist into it. He drew his hand back immediately and released a string of curses. If this was some kind of joke, it wasn't funny.

And then he smelled it...smoke. With his cell inside the cab of his vehicle, he had no way to call for help. With smoke filling the room, he had no time.

The window.

He pulled his shirt over his nose and mouth before feeling his way over to the dresser. Smoke was already seeping through the cotton of his shirt, causing his nose and throat to burn. And then he heard a noise toward the back of the room.

The raccoon?

Was he seriously still holding onto the fantasy a raccoon was responsible for locking him into his own equipment shed?

Dismissing the noise as probably a scurrying mouse, he chucked furniture pieces out of the way as he cleared the path to the window. The dresser was heavy as hell. It had taken him and his brother to move it to the spot where it sat now, blocking his exit. It was tall, though. Could he topple it over?

And then a familiar, if faint, female voice cut through the smoke.

"Help me."

CLICK here to continue reading Kellan's story.

ALSO BY BARB HAN

Texas Firebrand

Rancher to the Rescue

Disarming the Rancher

Rancher under Fire

Rancher on the Line

Undercover with the Rancher

Rancher in Danger

Set-Up with the Rancher

Rancher Under the Gun

Taking Cover with the Rancher

Firebrand Cowboys

VAUGHN: Firebrand Cowboys

RAFE: Firebrand Cowboys

MORGAN: Firebrand Cowboys

NICK: Firebrand Cowboys

ROWAN: Firebrand Cowboys

TANNER: Firebrand Cowboys

KEITH: Firebrand Cowboys

TRAVIS: Firebrand Cowboys

KELLAN: Firebrand Cowboys

Don't Mess With Texas Cowboys

Texas Cowboy's Protection

Texas Cowboy Justice

Texas Cowboy's Honor

Texas Cowboy Daddy

Texas Cowboy's Baby

Texas Cowboy's Bride

Texas Cowboy's Family

Texas Cowboy Sheriff

Texas Cowboy Marshal

Texas Cowboy Lawman

Texas Cowboy Officer

Texas Cowboy K9 Patrol

Cowboys of Cattle Cove

Cowboy Reckoning

Cowboy Cover-up

Cowboy Retribution

Cowboy Judgment

Cowboy Conspiracy

Cowboy Rescue

Cowboy Target

Cowboy Redemption

Cowboy Intrigue

Cowboy Ransom

For more of Barb's books, visit www.BarbHan.com.

ABOUT THE AUTHOR

Barb Han is a USA TODAY and Publisher's Weekly Bestselling Author. Reviewers have called her books "heartfelt" and "exciting."

Barb lives in Texas—her true north—with her adventurous family, a poodle mix, and a spunky rescue who is often referred to as a hot mess. She is the proud owner of too many books (if there is such a thing). When not writing, she can be found exploring new cities, on a mountain either hiking or skiing depending on the season, or swimming in her own backyard.

Sign up for Barb's newsletter at www.BarbHan.com.

Printed in Great Britain
by Amazon